Ordnance Road L¹
Hertford Road
Enfield
9-710588

18. JUL 197

12. AUG

12. SEP

19 0

17. FEB

12. MA

27. MAR.

THE GIRL FROM THE CANDLE-LIT BATH

When Nan Mansfield arrives home to hear her husband, Roy, on the telephone arranging a clandestine meeting in Regent's Park, she is determined to find out what he is involved in. Is there another woman – or can it be blackmail, drugs, even treason?

Roy is a Member of Parliament who was helped into politics by Cyprian Slepe, a brilliant eccentric who lives with his sister, Celina, in a decaying Stately Home. Nan comes to believe that Cyprian is connected with Roy's mysterious activities. Helped by an enigmatic taxi-driver she delves deeper and deeper, while her love and loyalty war with her ever-increasing suspicions, until at last she discovers that her own life is in jeopardy.

Though this fast-moving novel is a new departure for Dodie Smith, she brings to it all the skill at creating life-like and likeable characters which her loyal readers have come to count on.

By Dodie Smith

Novels

I CAPTURE THE CASTLE
THE NEW MOON WITH THE OLD
THE TOWN IN BLOOM
IT ENDS WITH REVELATIONS
A TALE OF TWO FAMILIES
THE GIRL FROM THE CANDLE-LIT BATH

For Children

THE HUNDRED AND ONE DALMATIANS
THE STARLIGHT BARKING
THE MIDNIGHT KITTENS

Plays

AUTUMN CROCUS
SERVICE
TOUCH WOOD
CALL IT A DAY
BONNET OVER THE WINDMILL
DEAR OCTOPUS
LOVERS AND FRIENDS
LETTER FROM PARIS
I CAPTURE THE CASTLE
THESE PEOPLE: THOSE BOOKS
AMATEUR MEANS LOVER

Autobiography

LOOK BACK WITH LOVE
LOOK BACK WITH MIXED FEELINGS

THE GIRL FROM
THE CANDLE-LIT BATH

Dodie Smith

W. H. Allen · London
A Howard & Wyndham Company
1978

Copyright © Dodie Smith, 1978

This book or parts thereof may not
be reproduced without permission in writing.

Photoset, printed and bound
in Great Britain by
Redwood Burn Limited
Trowbridge & Esher for the Publishers,
W. H. Allen & Co Ltd,
44 Hill Street, London W1X 8LB

ISBN 0 491 0 2113 5

London Borough
of Enfield
Public Libraries

R77986

TAPE ONE

Wednesday, June 12th. 10.30 p.m.

As I came into the flat this evening I heard Roy talking on the telephone. Not wanting to interrupt him I closed the front door quietly and went towards the little room where I'm now sleeping. Just as I went in I heard him say, 'Right, then. Seven o'clock. The bridge by the giant cow-parsley.' Then I heard him replace the receiver and I only had just enough time to push my door to before he crossed the hall and went out, slamming the front door.

If this tape-recorder had been working inside my head, all it would have picked up would have been, 'How *could* he, how *could* he,' over and over again. It was the choice of place that got me down most, that place where we met so often before we were married. (We never did find out what the giant cow-parsley really is.) The fact that he was meeting someone didn't come as a frightful shock; I've been suspicious for weeks. But I couldn't have believed he could be so crass as to choose that place and call it by our name for it.

I got to the window just in time to see him come out of the house into the square. I thought he would take the taxi which was on the rank just across the road, but he didn't, although he was carrying the suitcase I'd left packed for him. He hurried out of the square and out of sight. I guessed he might not want the taxi-driver – I could see it was the one who often drove us – to know where he was going.

I have a new white coat he's never seen and a black velvet hat I bought for a wedding. He wasn't with me when I wore it and I never wear hats unless I have to, so I felt sure he wouldn't recognise me at the distance I intended to keep. As I clattered down the seventy-two stairs that lead up to our top flat I prayed no one would swipe the taxi – not that there are many taxi-takers in our decayed square. Anyway, it was still there. I told the driver to take me to Hanover Gate, Regent's Park, as fast as he could. Usually that's a chatty young driver, but he didn't chat then and apart from taking in that he was our usual driver I didn't give him a thought. I went on mentally raging against Roy and mentally pushing the taxi so that we could get there ahead of him. We did, too. When we reached the Outer Circle I could see no sign of him on the bridge.

At Hanover Gate I jumped out, paid the driver and dashed into the park, skirting the bridge quite widely and making for a tree I could hide behind. I was only half-way there when I saw Roy coming from Clarence Gate. He wasn't carrying the suitcase so I guessed he had a taxi waiting. I ran the rest of the way with my head averted from him, though he was too far away to see my face clearly. I got behind the tree before he reached the bridge.

There was someone waiting there. I only had a back view but I took in fair, almost shoulder-length hair, much brighter than mine, and an odd-looking trouser-suit. Then Roy arrived. I saw no sign of a greeting. He merely stood beside the trouser-suited figure – I swear it wasn't as long as a minute – and then both of them were off, Roy towards Clarence Gate and the other towards Hanover Gate.

I was utterly bewildered, both by the shortness of the meeting and the fact that Roy could be interested in a woman with obviously dyed hair – and he loathes trouser-suits on women. I started to run, hoping to get a look at the woman's face, but she was striding along at a tremendous pace and just as I reached the Outer Circle she shot across it and went out of Hanover Gate. I then saw my taxi was still waiting. I thought I'd take it and try to follow the woman. But as I ran towards it I somehow tripped and fell, wrenching my ankle. It hurt so much that I didn't feel I could get up.

The taxi-driver was with me in a few seconds. He told me to stay where I was while he examined my ankle – he said he could tell if it was broken. I didn't think it was, the pain was already going off a bit, but what with being jarred by the fall and, well, everything, I was feeling frightfully sick. So when he said my ankle seemed all right and he'd help me into the taxi, I told him I wouldn't get into it in case I was sick. He said I probably wouldn't be and, anyway, if there was one thing taxis were used to, it was people being sick in them. Then he practically lifted me into the taxi. I think it was astonishment that stopped me feeling sick.

Naturally, I took it for granted he was driving me home, but almost at once he turned into a mews at the back of a Regent's Park terrace. Then he pulled up outside a yellow door, got out and opened the taxi door and said, 'This is where I live. I'll give you a drink or some coffee. You're not fit to go home yet. You've had a bad shock.'

I was feeling too bemused to argue with him, also I didn't want to snub him. I must have already taken in that there was a warm kindliness about him – not that I was really thinking about him; I only started to when he opened the yellow front door into a very luxurious room almost lined with books. As if he'd read my thoughts he said, 'This posh place is only lent to me by some friends.' Then he helped me to the kind of sofa that costs hundreds – my ankle was so much better that I barely needed to limp – and asked if I'd have coffee or a drink. I said coffee, drinks never helped me – and then wondered what the coffee would be like. Good coffee's something I've got dependent on.

When he'd gone to the kitchen I took in the room: golden

brown carpeting, golden brown leather upholstery, dark yellow curtains, two walls of tightly-filled brass bookshelves; it was indeed posh. Then I was back in the park, seeing that meeting on the bridge. Why meet, just to dash away from each other?

Tim was back surprisingly soon – it was about that time he told me his name. He brought a tray with an Espresso coffee maker and a glass dish of sandwiches and said his help always left him something. I said he was lucky to have good help and he said she belonged to the married couple who have lent him the house and they'd paid her to keep an eye on it – and him – during the six months they were spending in America. While he was making the coffee I took in that he isn't a very young man, as I've always taken him to be from his back view in the taxi, when I'd mainly noticed his hair. It is a sort of dark Simple Simon mop, wild but quite clean-looking, too young for his face. I'd say he's in his middle thirties.

I took a sandwich and he kept on pressing them on me, saying I'd feel better if I ate. I said I now felt all right and my ankle had stopped hurting. He said, 'But what happened in the park must have been pretty shattering for you. It'll clear the air if I say I saw your husband arrive and what happened on the bridge.'

For a second I felt I ought to find some way of shutting him up but, instead, I found myself saying: 'But *nothing* happened on the bridge.'

He said, 'Oh, yes it did. You couldn't see from where you were, but I had a front view. Only I couldn't see what it was your husband handed over.'

'Do you mean he gave her something?'

Tim stared. 'Are you under the impression that was a woman? It was a man – and not a very young one, in spite of the flowing apricot mane. And he was unusually ugly. He passed quite close to me as he left the park and I noticed he had a particularly large nose. Were you expecting your husband to meet some woman?'

Again I felt I ought to end the conversation but again I found myself talking freely, telling how I'd heard Roy make the appointment and how he and I used to meet on the bridge and how strange he's been these last weeks. Then I managed to pull myself up and said it was probably all my imagination and I'd better go.

Tim said, 'I know. It's dawned on you that this is a peculiar conversation to be having with a taxi driver and you're being disloyal and what not. But just forget about that. You could be in a dangerous situation. I tell you I'm quite sure your husband handed over a letter or a small package.'

I said the first thing that came into my head. 'Oh, God, could it be something to do with drugs? Roy *has* been strange lately.'

'But he was doing the handing over, remember. I'd find it hard to believe he's taken to drug-peddling. Oh, there may be some perfectly innocent explanation. What matters now is that you should find out without arousing his suspicions. Will he be at the flat when you get back?'

I said no, he was going to his constituency for some meeting tomorrow – 'You do know he's a Member of Parliament? He won't be back until tomorrow evening.'

'Then you've got time to get your feelings under control. I take it you don't intend to have things out with him?'

I said I didn't see how I could. 'If there's some innocent explanation he'll never forgive me for suspecting him, and if he has got some secret——'

'Then he'll lie to you and be on guard against you or, worse still, tell you the truth and involve you. Forgive me for seeming impertinent but to what extent would you stand by him?'

'Well, if he was taking drugs, not peddling them——'

'I'm quite sure he isn't taking them,' said Tim. 'Remember I've driven him again and again these last weeks and I swear I'd know. Drug-taking's something I'm up in. I researched the whole subject for my second book. I only drive a taxi six months of the year. The rest of the time I'm a thriller writer.'

He got up and took a book from a cupboard, saying his books weren't classy enough to rub shoulders with his friends' books on the shelves. The title of the novel he handed to me was *Some of my Best Friends are Spies* and the jacket showed a hand putting something down what looked like a rabbit-hole.

I said, 'Are you hinting that Roy might be a spy?'

He said no, that just happened to be his latest book. Still, I'd better face the fact that spying was a possibility. 'Does your husband serve on any parliamentary committees connected with defence?'

'Not that I know of, but he never talks to me about his work. That's probably my fault for being so stupid.'

Tim said seriously, 'Do you really consider yourself stupid?'

'About some things I am. Lyn – that's my great friend, Lyn Lyndon – always says actresses ought to be a bit stupid about everything except their own work and they oughtn't to be too intelligent even about that. They ought to feel, rather than think, once they've acquired a basic technique.'

Tim asked when I was going to act again and I found he remembered me from the series I did on television over a year ago. I told him I'd given the stage up, hoping to be a help to Roy (God knows there was more to it than that, but no need to mention it). Then Tim said, 'Will you be telling your friend everything that's happened tonight?'

I said, 'I can't. She's in New York, opening in a play, this very night. But I don't think I would tell her, anyway. She might not keep it to herself.'

'Then will you tell anyone?'

I said there was no one else I'd even consider telling.

'Then you'll go over and over it in your mind. You might even give yourself away to your husband. And believe me, quite apart from causing trouble between you, that could lead to real danger. Let's look on the blackest side and say that treasonable espionage is involved. If his masters find out that you suspect——' Tim broke off, then said, 'You'll think I'm being melodramatic but they really can be ruthless.'

'Do you mean I could get bumped off, run over or something, like on television?'

'Let's not talk about that. But from every point of view you should keep this thing to yourself – apart from me; it's too late for that. And you're going to need a safety valve for when I'm not on hand. Have you ever used a tape-recorder?'

It so happens that I have. When Lyn and I first met, at Drama School, we both wanted to get rid of regional accents without falling over backwards into the kind of society voices some of the girls at the school had. We aimed at classless voices, combined with very good diction, and we found that listening to ourselves on a tape-recorder was a great help. Sometimes we read plays together, sometimes we just talked, and then listened to see how often we had slid back into Midland accents. When I told Tim about this and said I still had our little machine and some unused tapes, he said I ought to go home and start talking, recording everything that happened tonight while it was fresh in my mind and also digging up anything I could remember about Roy's behaviour these last weeks.

'Just talk, talk,' said Tim. 'Let the recorder take the place of the inner monologue you'll conduct otherwise. Do you know what I mean?'

I didn't quite, so he explained about how he has to resist inner monologue when he's inventing a book. 'You can seldom remember what you've heard in your head and when you come actually to write you find a lot of the creative energy has vanished. I create best at the point of a pencil, but if inner monologue batters at me too much I dash to a tape-recorder and get some of it down for future use. And I record things I notice while driving, interesting settings, odd little incidents. Now in your case, as well as storing up facts, recording should help to stop you brooding, give you the kind of relief you get when you pour out your troubles to a friend.'

I got the idea at once. I could imagine myself sorting out these last weeks, trying to find clues in Roy's behaviour and having a shot at understanding my own feelings – which, God knows, are confused.

Tim asked if there was somewhere I could hide my recordings and I said they would be quite all right in my old theatrical basket, with a lot of the others I'd still got. There was a padlock on the basket and, anyway, I couldn't imagine Roy taking the slightest interest in it or anything to do with me. Tim gave me a quick look so I went on, 'Well, I *have* been resentful, but if he has something serious on his mind I ought to be more understanding.'

'Depends what it is,' said Tim. 'I suppose it could be that he's being blackmailed.'

'But what for? He's so ultra respectable.' That sounded deadly so I added, 'What I really mean is that he's a very good man.' Even that sounded a bit dreary.

Tim then said he would take me home so that I could have a bash at the tape-recorder, and he too wanted to do some work. 'I'll write down every explanation I can think of and bring the result tomorrow morning. You're sure your husband won't be back? Anyway, I'll take no risks. I'll park in the square at ten-thirty and I won't come up until you signal that the coast is clear.'

When I got up to go I could just feel the strain in my ankle, but nothing to worry about. While Tim put the lights off in the kitchen I took a last look round the room. It really is fascinating, with its shining brass bookshelves, many books with gold tooling on their backs, yellow-shaded lamps and some beautiful golden glass. Tim said he was frightened of breaking something and was thankful he didn't smoke. I hadn't noticed this, probably because I don't myself, neither does Roy.

I asked if I could borrow the thriller he'd shown me and on the drive home I got him to talk about his work. I didn't say I hadn't heard of him, but no doubt he took it for granted as I did say I seldom read thrillers. He told me his books do quite well – he's written three – and the sales go up a little with each book, but only half-a-dozen writers make real money out of thrillers and detective novels, and he's lucky to earn four or five hundred out of a book. But he likes writing and can turn out a book in six months. He wouldn't like to do two a year and he finds taxi-driving interesting and it helps him to get ideas.

I was thinking, 'Well, this evening will probably come in useful,' when he said, 'But don't imagine I'll be writing about what happened tonight. My last novel was about spying and my next one won't be – it's already planned. Not, of course, that I'm taking it for granted that Mr Mansfield really is connected with espionage.'

I said, 'God, no. He *can't* be,' and thought how staggering it was that I should suspect Roy of – well, anything really wrong. I've always felt I had my work cut out to live up to his standards.

Tim wouldn't let me pay for the drive home; he said he was off duty. He helped me out of the taxi and came up the front steps with me, and, while I was finding my key, said 'Don't you mind going into a pitch dark house like this?' I told him there were lights one could switch on, though they don't stay on long enough to see me up to the flat.

He looked at the brass plates on the door. 'Is yours the

only residential flat?'

I said yes, a solicitor has the two floors below us and someone imports something in the ground floor and basement. 'The whole house is getting pretty decrepit. When Roy bought the flat last year, before we married, he had an idea the square was going up, but it's still going down.'

'Too many people who can't be evicted, no doubt,' said Tim. 'I'll come right up to the flat with you. Sometimes there are lurkers in this type of house.'

'That's just the thriller writer in you. The last person to leave the solicitor's office always closes the front door of the house against lurkers.'

'Unless they get in before the door's closed,' said Tim as we went in.

I switched the lights on. As we went up Tim tried all the doors. Everything was locked except one door on the third floor which opens into what was once a bathroom. All that remains now is a lavatory and a decrepit washbasin. 'Just the place for someone to lurk in,' said Tim. Then the light went out.

'I ought to have brought my torch from the taxi,' said Tim. 'And you ought to have a pocket torch in your bag. I'll bring you one tomorrow. I loathe these lights that switch themselves off – though they're very useful to thriller writers. You can always work up suspense on a suddenly dark staircase. It's been overdone in books, but life doesn't mind repeating itself.'

There was no one lurking on the narrow stairs that lead up to the flat, but even when I'd opened the door Tim wasn't satisfied. He said, 'Mind if I look round?' and was inside, switching on lights, before I'd time to answer. I laughed and said, 'Tim, really! What are you expecting to find?'

'Oh, I'm being a thriller writer again.' He went into the kitchen, looked out of the window at the fire escape, and asked if it went all the way down. I told him the last section could be pushed down from above, but could not be reached from below. He said, 'Good,' then looked into every room in the flat and finished up by inspecting the two bolts on the front door and asking if I used them. I said never.

'Well, use them tonight. Seriously, you might be involved in something dangerous, though probably not yet. I shall feel better when I've had the chance to think hard about it. See you tomorrow at ten-thirty – if you give me the go-ahead. Good night, Mrs Mansfield.'

I said, 'I call you "Tim". Please reciprocate with "Nan"'

He said, 'Thank you, but I'd better not, in case it slipped out some day when I happen to be driving both you and Mr Mansfield. Though I don't think it will matter if he hears you call me Tim; lots of my regular customers do.'

Then he gave me his particularly nice, direct smile and I opened the door for him and switched on the staircase lights. I heard him close the door downstairs just after they switched themselves off.

I went in and shot both the front door bolts – not that I really believed I was in any danger – then I went to make some tea. Just after I'd made it, I heard a car in the mews at the back of the house. I don't remember ever hearing one before. At our end there are only little lock-up workshops and the other end's slum property, no bijou residences. So I went out onto the fire escape and looked down. There was someone with a torch just below. I felt a sudden clutch of fear. Then I saw it was Tim, making sure the bottom section of the fire escape wasn't down. Well, God bless him, but I think he must be a bit of an alarmist.

I carried my tea into my room, got the tape-recorder out of my theatrical basket and put on a new tape. I always get a pang when I look in that basket. I really ought to throw the junk in it away and use it to keep clothes in. This room's so small that, apart from the basket, my bed and a chair, I've only managed to get in the little painted chest-of-drawers I had when I shared Lyn's flat. Of course most of my clothes are still in the big bedroom, but it's a curse having to keep on diving in for them——

Oh, God, I've just thought of something – I suppose it's the kind of thing Tim hoped I'd remember. Isn't it a bit suspicious that Roy wanted to be on his own? I thought it was all part of his loss of interest in me and he was using his restlessness as an excuse. But it wasn't only his restlessness. He made the suggestion after I told him he'd been talking in his sleep. He asked what he'd said and I told him there had been nothing coherent except that he'd shouted 'No!' again and again. After that, he said he didn't want to disturb me and he'd use the little room, but I couldn't let him do that as there's only a 2ft 6 inch bed. Actually, I was glad to move in here because it was awful being . . . well, near him and not near him. Besides, his restlessness was hell, and once he fetched me a frightful swipe in his sleep – not that I ever told him.

He was very apologetic about letting me sleep in here; he said everything would be all right when he'd had a real rest and we must plan a holiday when the House goes into recess.

Oh, my poor Roy, are you in some frightful trouble and me doing nothing to help you? But I was so sure there must be another woman and I didn't feel I could do anything about that in case I brought everything into the open and we broke up. I just hoped things would get better.

And now what am I to do? Watch you, spy on you? Can I make myself believe in you, loyally? Surely, if one loves someone . . . But do I love him? This time yesterday I'd have sworn I did but . . .

Come on now, be honest. These last weeks have made a difference. And even earlier, months ago really . . . I've blamed myself for stupidity. Of course I don't really understand politics, but I do try to. I work hard on reading newspapers and looking at television, and if only he'd talk to me . . . But he says he doesn't want to talk about his work.

Of course I haven't stopped loving him because of some silly little mystery and because a taxi-driver's put melodramatic ideas into my mind! That's unfair to Tim. I like him, I trust him, I'm grateful to him. But he *is* a thriller writer with his head full of spies and what not.

I'm getting near the end of this tape. Tim was right. I have found talking a relief, almost like a long telephone talk to Lyn – except that she'd have kept on interrupting. I wonder how she's getting on tonight. Let's see, New York's five hours back so the curtain won't be up yet. Thank God I sent her a cable of good wishes before all this blew up. She'll be in her dressing-room. Hello, Lynnie! Well, you never did like Roy, did you? But you can't any longer call him a stuffed shirt, can you? Not if he's a spy, or something dashing . . . I can just hear your voice saying, 'Well, he can be a stuffed spy, can't he?'

Tape ending.

TAPE TWO

Thursday, June 13th. 9.30 a.m.

I've put in a new tape, my last; I must get some more today. I've played back all I said last night. As usual, my voice didn't sound like my voice to me, but I got used to it. I'm amazed how much I said in half-an-hour, even with pauses to think. Of course I haven't got in everything. Tim warned me I shouldn't be able to remember conversations exactly. But I do have a retentive ear and I think it will get more retentive with practice, especially if I cut out most of the 'he saids and she saids' and just *listen* – which is the way I usually remember conversations.

I read some of Tim's book in bed last night and over breakfast this morning. It's very well-written but I shouldn't have thought it was thrilling enough for a thriller. It's more real than I expected, with a lot of detail about how spies work, how they hand over their information and use codes. My mind goes off duty when it's faced with codes and I'd decided the book was a bit dull, when it suddenly got fascinating, all about queer little backstreets surprisingly close to the West End of London, and then a highly respectable suburb where, I gather, sinister things are going to happen. I can see why driving a taxi helps Tim's imagination.

I slept better than I expected to and woke up feeling less miserable than I expected to. Anyway, it was a less leaden kind of misery than has descended on me every morning for weeks, more interesting and less humiliating. It doesn't now seem as if Roy is in love with someone else and, though I'd rather he was than involved in spying or blackmail or drugs – I believe I really do mean that – I feel less hurt.

I'm going to dash out now and buy more tapes. I can be back before Tim gets here.

11.40 a.m.
I got home just as Tim arrived in his taxi, but he refused to come up until I'd made sure Roy hadn't returned, and then signalled to him. He arrived at the front door holding a lady's handbag, saying it would provide a reason for his visit should Roy turn up unexpectedly, the idea being that the bag had been left in the taxi and Tim thought it might be mine. I'd have to say I'd taken the taxi the previous evening to go to a film, and Tim made me decide where I'd been, so that I could sound convincing. He was dead serious about it, and he'd gone to the trouble of filling the bag with the kind of things women have in handbags, including a tiny torch which he made me keep. The bag will come with him whenever he comes to the flat, but he wants to avoid coming. I said it would be quite safe when Roy was away, in his constituency, or on the Continent where he goes for a few days every few weeks.

Tim pounced on the Continent. 'What does he go for? Parliamentary business?'

'No, it's to do with his own business. He has one, in his constituency. It's an old family business, something to do with leather – and plastics, now. I don't know much about it.'

'Just as you don't know much about his parliamentary work.'

'Well, I told you I was stupid.'

Tim surprised me by saying, 'I think you are, a bit. Oh, not in the way you mean. No one could believe you weren't intelligent. But hasn't it dawned on you that he doesn't *intend* you to know much about him?'

'Well, I told you last night. He doesn't like talking about his work. I suppose he feels the need for recreation.'

'And do you share recreations? Go out together, visit friends? How about the weekends?'

'He often spends them in his constituency. I sometimes went with him when his mother was alive and we could stay with her. She died six months ago and now he stays in a hotel and says it's pointless for me to come with him.' I suddenly felt quite awful. I was presenting Tim with a marriage that was breaking up – and I've never let myself believe that, not even during these last weeks.

Tim was looking at me closely, with those kind eyes which are so much older than his boyish mop of hair. Then he looked away and said quite lightly, 'Well, see what I've come up with in the way of ideas.'

We were in the kitchen. I'd been making coffee. He drank his while I read his notes. They were handwritten, in a tiny but very legible hand. He *is* an astonishing person. His neat handwriting seems so unsuited to his appearance and personality; his hair and his clothes are sloppy and so is his speech. He has no particular accent but his diction is pretty well non-existent, his words tumble out in a general blur – though he has quite a pleasant voice.

He told me to burn his notes and so I will, once I've recorded them – not that I'm likely to forget them.

TIM'S NOTES

Problem: A Member of Parliament (in his early thirties?) entered the House last year as member for a safe Conservative seat, Midlands industrial constituency, handsome, civil to taxi-driver, reasonably good tipper, meets by appointment a man (thirtyish, ugly, conspicuous long, fair hair) in Regent's Park. These two stand side by side, for less than a minute, and something is handed over by the M.P. Then they part, apparently without speaking to each other and without even looking at each other. M.P. leaves in direction of Baker Street, other man leaves in direction of St John's Wood. Time: soon after 7 p.m.

POSSIBLE EXPLANATIONS

1. Espionage. (Treasonable)
2. Espionage. (Industrial)
3. Drugs.
4. Blackmail.
5. Sex – Another Woman.
6. Sex – A Man.
7. An Innocent Explanation.

AMPLIFICATIONS

Treasonable Espionage: 'They' – presumably, but not necessarily, the Russians – would probably be willing to recruit any M.P. willing to be recruited. M.P. is not known to be connected with Defence, but one gets the impression that 'they' can find interest in the most trivial information (the price of buns in the House of Commons tea-rooms?) if it is considered *inside* information. However, once they have a recruit, they will sooner or later require important information. Suspect may have prospect of acquiring some, such as output of various industries.

Industrial Espionage: I know less about this as it's hardly material for a thriller writer. But the fact that it strikes me as dull doesn't prevent it happening, sometimes involving millions of pounds – and suspect is connected with industry. All the same, I can't quite feel it would involve such cloak-and-dagger effects as surreptitious meetings, handing over small packets, etc.

Drugs: Whatever was handed over by the M.P. could have been drugs, or payment for drugs. But neither his wife nor I can believe he takes them, and that he should peddle them seems to be more unbelievable than that he should be a spy.

Blackmail: This seems unlikely because of suspect's fine character and respectability. But is it any more unlikely than espionage or involvement with drugs?

Sex – Another Woman: (M.P.'s young wife, highly talented actress, no longer acting, suspected this.) At first this seemed to me out of the question because surely, in these days, he wouldn't have to make use of a go-between? But it is conceivable that the woman might fear her husband would open her letters, and suspect might fear his wife would open his, so meetings might have to be arranged by a go-between. This would, of course, mean a risk of blackmail and I doubt if I could make the go-between idea convincing in a novel. But life doesn't have to convince anybody.

Sex – A Man: As above, the idea of a go-between seems improbable, and personally I think it unlikely suspect is homosexual.

An Innocent Explanation: So far, I haven't come up with one, but I'm working on it.

The first thing I said after reading Tim's notes was 'How ghastly to think of one's husband as "the suspect".'

Tim said I must face the fact that I did suspect my husband.

I said, 'Suppose I stop? Suppose I wrench my mind off the whole thing? Or suppose I concentrate on the other woman theory? That would hurt me, it *has* been hurting me, but at least it doesn't involve Roy in anything criminal.'

'Well, you can try to concentrate on that idea, but it won't make it true if it isn't true. And surely you need to protect yourself? If your husband's a spy or connected with drugs or blackmail you need to know.'

'But there *may* be an innocent explanation – and anyway, it may be over by now. Oh, God, I wish I'd never followed him.'

Tim was giving me a very straight look and I suddenly felt I couldn't stand it. I said, 'Forgive me and thank you for all you've done, but you'd better leave me to cope on my own.'

'Are you throwing me out?'

'No, not that but – well, surely you can see . . . ? Anyway, what can I do? You're not suggesting I should leave my husband?'

'That might indicate you knew too much, which could be dangerous. All I suggest is that you watch, and use your wits. And in case you do throw me out I'm going to say my say first. You strike me as being in a coma of inertia; I suspect you have been for months.'

It was so exactly the way I've been feeling that I could only stare at him blankly. He said, 'True?'

I suddenly felt I was going to cry. I swallowed hard and just nodded. Then I said, 'I won't throw you out and if I do, don't go. Oh, Tim, I need help and there's no one but you I can turn to.'

'Well, I'm honoured to be turned to. But have you no friends except Lyn Lyndon?'

'There's no one else I've kept up with. All my friends were in the theatre world and it's a world Roy dislikes – it's been none too easy keeping up with Lyn. Oughtn't you to get back to your taxi?'

'Not if there's anything I can do to help you.'

I said I'd obviously got to help myself now and I did find talking to the tape-recorder helpful. 'I'll have another session with it.'

'Show me where you're hiding the tapes.'

When we went into my room the recorder, with the tape I began early this morning, was still on the bed. Tim said I must never, never leave it out, even if I only went to answer the door bell. When I showed him the inside of my theatrical basket, he said that was quite a good hiding place, particularly if I put the new tapes under those Lyn and I made together. He picked up some of these and read how I had labelled them, *Shakespeare's Sonnets, Scenes from The School for Scandal, The Importance of Being Earnest,* then asked how I was going to label the new tapes. I said I hadn't planned to label them.

'You should. Otherwise they'll look conspicuous if anyone ever does search the basket. That's a feeble padlock.'

'I might call last night's tape *The Perplex'd Wife.* Isn't that a Restoration comedy?'

'You're thinking of Vanbrugh's *The Provok'd Wife.* I don't think there was a *Perplex'd Wife.*'

I said, 'Well, there is, now.'

Tim laughed but said, 'Seriously, I'd choose authentic titles, and back-date the labels, to fit with earlier ones.'

'I do assure you Roy would never take the slightest interest in any of my recordings.'

'I don't think you know Mr Mansfield very well, Mrs Mansfield. Anyway, he's not the only person who might be interested. Which reminds me, on no account should you follow him again. If you're once seen following him – well, just don't. Now it won't be safe for me to get in touch with you, but you can ring me in the very early morning or after eight in the evening. I'm usually home by then and I'll make a point of it this week. Can you memorise the number?'

'Not reliably. Can't I write it down?'

Tim looked round the room and noticed a framed photograph of Lyn on the mantelpiece. He took the photograph out of the frame and wrote a string of figures on the back of it, then said, 'There! That looks like some photographer's reference number. If you discard the first three figures and the last three, you'll find my number in between them.'

It occurred to me that I may end up writing to him in code and putting my letters under stones. But there's no doubt that he's dead serious. He put the photograph back in its frame, then put my recorder into the basket, closed the lid and the padlock, and asked where I kept the key. I said in the chest of drawers. He said, 'Well, don't. Put it in your handbag and always take it out with you. Now I'm off.'

I told him it was quite time, and I must be preventing him from earning his living. He said not to worry, he was feeling rich. His last thriller had been sold for a paperback, the first paperback offer he'd had. It then dawned on me that I hadn't said a word about his book so I told him I was enjoying it and would probably finish it over lunch. He asked if I was eating properly. He thought I was too thin.

I said, 'You *can't* be too thin.'

'Oh yes you can, in the face.'

'Thanks for the hint. I'll start stuffing myself.'

'And isn't there any drink that gives you a lift? You said last night that drink never helped you, but surely there must be something . . .'

I told him I dislike the taste of spirits, and sherry and wine make me feel heavy. 'I always drink a little at parties because it's so boringly conspicuous not to, but the only drink I really like is champagne.'

'Have you got any?'

'Heavens, no. We never entertain here.'

'Well, you ought to have *something* to cheer you up.'

I said coffee was my dope and I could drink it six times a day. Tim said it was very bad for the complexion. 'Makes it leathery.' I *think* he meant it as a joke.

After he'd gone I went and looked at myself in the glass. I have the kind of face you can flatter by referring to beauty of bone structure – at my best I faintly resemble Greta Garbo. At my worst I strongly resemble a famine victim. The famine victim is winning out at present. But damn it, you couldn't call my skin leathery.

Then I started to talk to the recorder. I wonder why I find it so comforting. It's not a bit like talking aloud to oneself.

I've found myself doing that sometimes since Lyn went to New York; we used to talk every day on the telephone. I believe talking to oneself is a sign of approaching dottiness, but talking to the recorder makes me feel saner. I'm going to spend a fortune on tapes . . . Pause for thought. It's not only the talking that helps. I like to feel that what I've said exists – I couldn't bear to strip the tapes and use them again. Anyway, part of Tim's plan was that I should keep them for reference. And he thought I might unearth something useful. I haven't, so far – except about Roy talking in his sleep. But perhaps if I dig into the past . . . I'll have a shot at that later. I rather fancy it.

How extraordinary that I should have made friends with Tim yesterday, and what a blessing! How should I feel now if I'd seen what I saw in the park and just come home to brood about it? I'm desperately thankful for Tim. Surely he's a most unusual person? I've been wondering – damn, there's the door bell. . . .

When I opened the front door there was no one there, but I could hear someone clattering down the stairs. And there was a carrier bag on the mat with a half bottle of champagne in it. I got to the window in time to see Tim dash to his taxi and drive away. How terribly kind! I could weep. But I'm not going to. I'm going to do just what he'd want me to: get a good meal. I'm suddenly hungry.

TAPE THREE

Thursday, June 13th (continued). 6.00 p.m.

All I could find was a tin of Spam – I bet the champagne was snooty about being served with it. But I ate the whole tin and enjoyed it. Since then, I've been out shopping, I never keep much food in the house as Roy despises tinned and frozen foods – he says all he asks for is 'a simple steak', as if that was a most modest request – but I've no right to run out of eggs. I've been going to pieces about food, largely because Roy's so often out; he's always saying he'll get 'a bite' at the House of Commons. Now, anyway, I've stocked up on simple steaks for him and tinned and frozen foods for unfussy me. But tonight *I'll* have a simple steak, with the rest of the champagne.

As I'm still in the mood for self-delving, here goes: How does a reasonably attractive, reasonably intelligent woman, not long ago on the way to being rather more than reasonably successful as an actress, land herself in a coma of inertia? And I was pretty well in one before I followed Roy yesterday.

Think back: Dull but fairly happy childhood. Very dear invalid mother, crippled by the car accident that killed my father. I could never have left home, but she wasn't helpless and I was able to hold down a job in a Midhampton department store, old-established; we'd been good customers there before my father was killed, everyone was pleasant to me. I liked selling but I longed to act, ever since one miraculous visit to London when I was ten years old. I played a few times with local amateurs, but it meant spending too many evenings away from mother. I was twenty-two when she died, late for starting to train for the stage, and there wasn't much money. She'd had an annuity, bought with the damages she was awarded after the car accident, but of course that ended with her death. But she'd saved three hundred pounds to leave me and I'd saved another hundred. I went straight to London and managed to land a scholarship at a Drama School – oh, not one of the top schools, it's gone bust now, but I learnt quite a lot and I met Lyn. She knew more about looking for work than I did and we both got tiny parts in a play that was going on a long tour before coming to London. I suppose we were unusually lucky but it was a large cast, we weren't bad-looking, and we weren't expensive.

The tour was sent out by Richard Gott, already successful as a manager, but much more so now. He was nice to me whenever he joined the tour and even nicer after we opened in London. I liked him, too. He's still in his thirties and quite attractive, though a bit too heavy. Thick dark hair, thick glasses, a sardonic manner but very kind-hearted. And, let's face it, successful managers have a built-in charm for ambitious young actresses. I was attracted all right, though I kept on telling Lyn I wasn't in love with him. She told me not to split hairs but just get on with it, and that even if I had had to spare my invalid mother's feelings, a virgin rising twenty-five was an anachronism, not to mention a freak. So – well, I find I've no desire to go back over it all, though I was quite happy about it and it made life more exciting. We weren't really together very much. He has a complicated home life, with a very nice wife and children; I never felt guilty towards her because I knew I'd had predecessors. Lyn and I went on sharing our comic flat. Rich liked her very much. He gave her almost as many presents as he gave me, and never let her feel out of things. The play was doing well and it was always understood he'd have more work for us, as he has had for Lyn. What happened to me was that, just before the play finished its year's run, I got a chance in television.

It began with something quite idiotic. I did a very well-paid commercial, advertising a soap first made back in the eighteen-nineties. They copied a wonderful bathroom in some old country house, with a marble bath, gleaming silver plumbing and all sorts of elaborate details, and they lit it only by candle-light. I came on in an exquisite negligée, took it off and stepped into the bath, but owing to the dim lighting, clever cutting and various tricks, I was never seen *quite* nude, even though the bath water was clear and not a bubble bath. Again and again I was almost seen but always something – usually the soap, in a silver soap dish – got in the way. The commercial was a great success and I became known as 'The Girl in the Candle-lit Bath' and got quite a large fan mail.

Then I got a tiny part in a television play, and I think critics were astonished that I could speak presentably. (I never spoke a word in the commercial, never smiled or looked at the camera; the idea was that I was just having a private bath.) Anyway, I got several good notices, and then I got a much better part in a series that lasted three months, and then I was in some quizzes. So that in less than a year I was becoming quite well-known. Meanwhile, Lyn got a goodish part in another play of Rich's. It's still running, but she's left the cast to play the lead in the American production – an enormous chance for her; Rich arranged it. Lyn's much cleverer than I am. I do wonder how she got on last night. I might ring Rich up this evening; he'll know about the important notices by then. But I'm still inhibited about getting in touch with him – for his sake as well as Roy's.

Not until I had to break things off with Rich did I realise how fond of me he was. I'd taken it for granted that I was simply one of a succession. But according to Lyn, I haven't had a successor.

Although Roy and I were both of us born and brought up in Midhampton, we didn't meet until over three years after I had come to London. But I knew of him and of his family firm, and I sometimes served his mother. Once when I carried some parcels out to the car for her he was in the driver's seat, but he didn't notice me. It must have been four or five years after that when he won the by-election and I saw him on television. He has the kind of good looks which suggest an eighteenth-century painting; it would suit him to have his thick, fair hair tied back with a velvet ribbon; not that he wears it long and it's too tidy to be 'with it'. Indeed, he's too well-groomed to be fashionable. But he's not stodgily old-fashioned.

When I saw him on television I had a faintly proprietary feeling because we both came from Midhampton, though from different backgrounds. Actually, those backgrounds weren't so very different before my father died and mother and I went lower in the social scale whereas Roy rose higher, mainly because he was taken up by Cyprian and Celina Slepe, our local aristocrats. They are brother and sister, decorative, eccentric and, in my opinion, detestable. One has no right to detest people one hasn't met, but one's entitled to detest their public personality, especially when there's too much of it, as there is with the Slepes. Still, I know Roy owes them a lot. Without them, he'd still be an ordinary Midhampton business man – no, that's not true. If he'd been ordinary, surely the Slepes wouldn't have taken him up, got him interested in politics and helped him nurse the constituency.

He and I first met in Regent's Park; I used to call it our park pick-up. I recognised him at once – it was soon after I'd seen him on television. He'd seen me too, though he didn't then remember that and merely thought my face was familiar. Anyway, we stared at each other and then I explained who I was and we talked about Midhampton and what had been happening to us; it was a case of local boy and girl make good and congratulate each other. I don't say we fell in love at first sight, but we were certainly attracted as we arranged to meet again the next morning, on that bridge by the giant cow-parsley.

We went on meeting there. He was living with the Slepes in their flat near Baker Street and didn't feel he could ask me there and I didn't like to ask him home because Rich was liable to drop in unexpectedly. Anyway, in little more than a week we knew we were in love and would have to straighten things out. Roy was in a difficult position. The Slepes were possessive. I imagined he had been having an affair with Celina and, though he said it had never been quite that, whatever it was had been going on for a long time. And there was no doubt that the Slepes were important to his career. They had got him where he was and intended to get him much further. They'd taken the flat so that they could entertain for him in London as well as have weekend parties at the Hall; they said it was all a question of his knowing the right people. Cyprian's a very clever political journalist when he feels like it. The anti-Slepe faction in Midhampton used to call him a Fascist.

This was no moment for Roy to present me to his patrons as his future wife and we discussed the possibility of giving each other up. It was I who put it into words as I felt Roy would loathe saying his career was more important to him than I was. I tried to make things easier by saying I didn't want to hurt Rich, and *he* was important to *my* career. Though I felt I'd have to break with him anyway, now I was in love with Roy and, as for my career, I'd got into television entirely on my own. Actually, bringing Rich into it was a mistake as it made Roy jealous of him and, in a way, jealous of my having a career. And though he doesn't quite admit it,

I'm sure he thinks of the stage as a disreputable life in which women have to sleep with managers to get parts. I wasn't in too good a position to refute this. It made things more difficult for me when, quite suddenly, Roy felt free to marry me.

What happened was that the Slepes decided to leave England, possibly for ever, and with the utmost publicity – they have a genius for getting publicity. England was hopeless, Income Tax, Inflation, a wretched government and there was nothing to be done about it. They sold the flat and closed the Hall. No, they weren't handing it over to the National Trust, which expected to be *paid* to accept one's most treasured possession. Anyway, they hated the idea of the public tramping over beautiful old houses, which should be private, part of their owners' private lives. If the Slepes ever acquire a private life they'll be bitterly disappointed. They don't mind what the papers say about them as long as they say it, with plenty of photographs. Both of them are highly photogenic. They are very fair, with heads too small for their tall, thin bodies but their features are exquisite. Cyprian's thirty-seven, Celina's thirty-five. They've never married and there's a school of thought that says they're incestuous.

Roy says he never told them about me, but I've sometimes wondered if he did, or if they somehow found out and it stopped them from feeling guilty about leaving him high and dry – which they certainly did. Apart from their having undertaken to further his career, he had nowhere to live. It was then that he took this flat. You almost always have to buy flats now so the chance of renting one for a short lease seemed miraculous, even though the rent's high for this dreary locality. We call it Camden Town, but even that's flattering it. All that mattered to me was that Roy now felt free to marry, which we did as soon as the Slepes were out of England. When he wrote and told them, Cyprian replied on a postcard saying: 'Splendid news! Good luck to you, dear boy.' Roy says that the terseness indicates how much they mind, but I wonder.

The person who really did mind was Rich, though he said very little about it and behaved quite beautifully. Roy even resented my feeling sympathetic and asked me not to see Rich again, which meant I had to refuse a part Rich had lined up for me. However, I could have gone on with television. I then discovered Roy really wanted me to give up acting altogether; and what with feeling guilty because Roy so resented my affair with Rich, and wondering if I was in some way to blame for the loss of the Slepes, I agreed. I told myself I could be happy just helping Roy, seeing he was well looked after, entertaining for him. I really felt willing to . . . at first. How long did that last?

I've just played back all I've recorded this evening. God, this machine's revealing. Again and again my voice sounds spiteful and not only about the Slepes. I sound spiteful – well, anyway, resentful – about Roy. And I suddenly know I've been fooling myself in believing it's only since he started behaving so strangely to me that I've felt resentful. I've felt it for months. Perhaps he's noticed it. Perhaps I'm the one to blame.

I think the trouble is that I've been so abysmally bored. He's given me no chance to entertain for him. He's once or twice mentioned asking some fellow M.P. to dine at the club Cyprian got him into, but I don't believe he has a circle of friends – unless he's keeping them from me, as he keeps his work. Perhaps he feels I'm too stupid to understand it, but I do keep abreast of the political news and I think I could keep my end up. Incidentally, I never see his name mentioned. He doesn't seem to take part in debates, ask questions . . . Of course, lots of back-benchers don't, but it does seem odd that he's been in the House over a year, and he attends regularly, and yet he's never made his maiden speech. He was planning to make it last autumn, just before the Slepes left England. The only time I spoke of it to him he said there was no point in speaking until he had something he particularly wanted to say, and then changed the subject. Why, why won't he talk to me about his work?

I hear Lyn's voice saying, 'Because he has nothing to say. He's a stuffed shirt, darling. I warned you.' . . . It's not true. *I'm* the one at fault. I shouldn't have let myself get bored. Bored people are boring. No wonder he doesn't want to discuss anything with me.

I'm not going to talk any more now. Today it's making me feel worse, not better.

9.50 p.m.

I cheered up after I'd had my steak and the rest of Tim's champagne, and soon after eight I rang him to thank him for it. He hasn't been back in the square all day or I'd have gone down. Now he's told me not to, unless I actually need a taxi. It seems far-fetched that anyone round here would notice if I had a chat with a taxi-driver, but Tim was firm about it. He says that in an emergency I can go down, hail him, and we'll talk while he drives me somewhere. Not that I can count on his being in the square. Today he had a long out-of-town job.

When I told him how depressed I'd felt this evening, he said that was a good thing, as it meant I was digging out the truth about my own feelings as well as past happenings. He asked, very tentatively, if I'd let him listen to the tapes. I didn't feel I could do that but I gave him a rough idea of what I'd said about coming to London, meeting Roy, etc. He was particularly interested in the Slepes, about whom he seemed to know quite a lot – well, who doesn't? He said that if Roy had been influenced by them it didn't at all fit with his being connected with espionage, spies usually being Communist-oriented. I said anyway Roy hadn't seen them since they left England last autumn.

Tim said couldn't I come round? I'd have loved to but there was just a chance Roy might get back from his constituency around nine, instead of waiting for the later train. Then Tim and I talked about ordinary things, like my steak dinner and his book – I've nearly finished it. He suddenly said, 'It's five to nine. You must ring off and prepare to behave normally.'

I did, until half-past-nine. Then, as Roy hadn't arrived, I knew he wouldn't be back until nearly midnight. So I got into a dressing-gown and settled down to this recording.

All the time I was talking to Tim I visualised him in that brown and gold room. It *is* a bit unlived in, a tiny showcase of a room, but everything in it was pleasant to look at. Thinking about it made me see how awful this flat is. When Roy took it he had to accept its carpets, curtains and a good deal of furniture Midhampton shops describe as 'contemporary'. Then, when his mother died, he inherited her furniture – which no doubt was 'contemporary' in her youth. Roy felt we should keep some. That means that the flat is crowded with ugliness, but there seems nothing to be done about it until we move and refurnish, as we originally planned to. But Roy seems less and less keen on this.

11.30 p.m.

I broke off because, again, talking was making me feel depressed – and indignant. Since then I've been watching television and was treated to a play in which Special Branch, or anti-spies of some kind – turned a flat upside down, looking for a secret radio. It was inside an immersion heater that wasn't an immersion heater. Then someone got shot. I'm always noticing in television plays about espionage that the anti-spies never have to explain corpses to the police. I think there must be a corpse-sweeping department that moves in and gets rid of the bodies. I can't believe that Roy has anything to do with such a world – or that quite such a world exists.

I must now put this machine away. Roy should be back very soon.

TAPE FOUR

Friday, June 14th. 7.30 p.m.

Everything has changed! Oh, I wish I could have known last night, all those hours I lay awake.

When I heard his key in the door I went to meet him. He said I shouldn't have waited up – which I always do. I asked if I could get him something to eat and he said no; he just wanted to sleep. When he's tired he gets a vulnerable look that always harrows me.

I lay awake until four; I heard a clock strike. And then I didn't stir until ten o'clock when I opened my eyes to find him standing by my bed with a tray of breakfast. I was so dazed that for a minute I couldn't believe I was awake. Never has such a thing happened before. In our earliest days we sometimes had breakfast in bed, side by side, but I always got the trays, and though it was fun it was wildly inconvenient for reading the papers. For ages now we've got up to breakfast and for weeks we've taken refuge in reading.

This morning, Roy smiled when he set the tray down; then he said he had a bath running and whisked away before I could say more than, 'What a lovely surprise.' I was so excited that I could hardly eat – and I must admit it was a frightful breakfast. The boiled egg had cracked and was full of water and the tea was so strong it looked like stout. And he'd used the top of the milk. I loathe cream in tea. Still, it was heaven.

I was ready to go into the bathroom when he came out. He said, 'Let's have a talk when you're dressed.' When I joined him in the sitting room I saw at once that he was looking better. His eyes are very wide apart and when he's at his best they have a smiling serenity. They hadn't quite got that, but they were more lively than I've seen them for months.

He said something nice about my dress, which he's seen several times before but never noticed. Then he said he'd been thinking that life had become very dull for me and he was afraid he'd been neglecting me. It was because he'd had a lot on his mind. I said I'd realised that and longed to help him, but he'd been quite a bit rebuffing.

He said, 'I know. But I find it difficult to talk about my worries, also I genuinely didn't want to burden you with them. Still, there are certain things you may as well know.'

I gradually gathered that one of his worries was the family business which he ought either to close or spend more time with; it's mainly run by two of his uncles and it's beginning to lose money. Then he said he'd been troubled by some of his supporters in Midhampton who didn't feel he'd made himself felt politically. However, things would soon be better about that. I said 'Oh, good' most eagerly and was going to ask if he could tell me anything about his plans when he brushed the subject aside by saying, 'But let's forget about all these things now and go out to lunch – somewhere nice.' I said, 'How lovely' and decided not to press any questions on him. What he'd told me had been . . . well, almost enough to account for his strangeness, all except that meeting in Regent's Park, and the relief of having him talk to me of his own accord had driven that out of my head.

There was a taxi in the square, but mercifully it wasn't Tim's so I didn't have to put on any kind of an act. Roy had asked me where I'd like to lunch, but in all the restaurants I know well it was possible that we might run into Rich, so I said, 'You choose', and we ended up in a very stodgy place full of business men. Roy said you could always trust the food there. Like so many trustworthy things it was also a bit dull. For once Roy didn't order a steak – well, the price was astronomical – and I thought the beef was overdone. (He likes it that way). But I was too happy at being with Roy to take much notice of the food – not that you can eat not very tender beef without noticing it and the chewings are apt to kill conversation.

When we finished, he said he would like to go home, write some letters and then take a nap as he had an important evening ahead of him. He is entertaining some Midhampton business friends at his club and taking them out afterwards. So we got a taxi and drove home through the West End. I was careful not to look at the theatres – I always fall over backwards not to indicate any wistfulness for the stage – so I was astonished when Roy said, out of the blue, 'Have you seen Richard Gott lately?'

I said, 'Not since I married you, as you very well know. You asked me not to.'

He murmured something about not having meant that so definitely – 'I took it for granted you'd run into him sometimes, say when you go to see Lyn.'

'I make her warn him off when I'm coming. Not that he'd ever drop in on her without telephoning. Lyn has her own private life to lead.'

'And a very busy one, I'm sure.' He has an idea that Lyn is very, very busy as regards men. Well, she is fairly busy.

The taxi got held up within sight of Rich's theatre. I had a sudden wave of nostalgia. And at that moment Roy said, 'Would you like to go back to the stage? Oh, not full-time, perhaps. I daresay television would be better. I shouldn't mind if you made an occasional appearance. I'm so often at the House in the evenings.'

I said, and I hope I didn't sound deliberately patient, 'Roy, dear, if one does a television play the rehearsals and recordings take place in the daytime and they go on for several weeks – and much longer, if you get into a series. You don't just drop in to the studios of an evening without preparation.'

'*I* did.'

'Well, that was because of your election – and even then, you were recorded.'

'They've never asked me to appear again. Though I was all right, wasn't I?'

'You were splendid. But there's never been any particular reason since——' I suddenly felt I was on dangerous ground. 'They'll ask you soon enough when next you're in the public eye.'

'I need to be, don't I? I must do something about it. Though in a way, one has a horror of publicity.'

I had a flash of understanding. He does dislike publicity. It's to do with his upbringing. I remember when I used to serve his mother, again and again she would turn down clothes because they were 'too conspicuous'. I think I've always known he would never have stood for parliament if he hadn't somehow been galvanised by Cyprian Slepe.

I said, 'Naturally, I never had such a horror or I wouldn't have wanted to act. Do you really mean you won't mind if I go back to work?'

'Not if it'll make you happy. But I think I'd prefer it to be the theatre, not television. Television's so very public. Millions of people see you.'

'Well, so one hopes. But I like the stage better. My bit of success on television was just a fluke.' The taxi was moving again; I felt sorry to let the theatres go. And then I felt I had to say something which might queer everything. 'You do realise I shall have to talk to Richard Gott? He's my only important contact in the theatre.'

After a moment's silence Roy said, 'Yes, all right. I think I've been unreasonable about him. From what you've told me he's a very decent chap.'

He is indeed, though that's the last way I'd describe him. And Roy wouldn't either if he knew about my predecessors. He still clings to his family's rigid standards about morals.

When we got home he went to lie down; nothing more was said about letter-writing. I drew the curtains and turned down the bed while he got into his dressing gown. As I was leaving the room he held out his hand to me, but dropped it as I went towards him and just said, 'Sorry – about everything.'

I told him everything was all right now. 'There's nothing to be worried about.'

'Oh, yes, there is. But it'll be all right now.' He smiled very sweetly, then added, 'I hope.'

I longed to stoop and kiss him, but he wasn't inviting a kiss; in fact, he said very briskly, 'Wake me at seven if I haven't wakened.' I said, 'Right,' just as briskly, and went. I'm so anxious not to appeal for affection in case he takes it as a reminder that it's weeks – soon it'll be months – since we made love. What matters now is that things are on the way to coming right. I mustn't try to hurry them.

I'd have liked to talk to this machine at once, while everything was fresh in my mind, but of course that was out of the question with Roy in the flat. I'd had enough lift of spirit to feel like going through my clothes, but most of them were shut up with Roy. So I lay on my bed and thought. There was something that made me even happier than the change in Roy; it was the change in my own feelings, the reawakening of them, that moment in the bedroom when he smiled at me. It made me realise that if I can care for him it's really more important than if he cares for me. It makes me feel able to believe in him, to push disloyal thoughts out of my mind.

I fell asleep and woke in a panic in case I'd let Roy oversleep. But it was only a little after six. Before I woke him, I stood looking down on him. I'm sure no one with that wide, untroubled brow could be involved in espionage or anything awful.

After he left the house (he took Tim's taxi) I rushed at this machine. Now I'm going to break off and see if I can arrange an appointment with Rich this very night. He's almost always in the theatre in the evenings.

I'm back from the telephone. Rich was somewhere backstage but his secretary said he has no appointments this evening and she's sure he'll see me. I said, 'Well, if he doesn't want to, just ring up.' She laughed and said, 'I shan't need to.' She was always nice to me. Today she said, 'How good to hear your voice again.' We arranged that I'd be there at ten.

Then I had an idea. Tim's taxi was back in the square. If I booked him to drive me to the theatre, we could talk on the way and I could tell him we must be wrong in suspecting Roy. So I went down to him. He didn't look pleased to see me and reminded me he'd asked me not to come down and talk. However, he agreed I had a legitimate reason. Then he saw a man approaching and said loudly 'Right, madam. I'll be here at nine-thirty.' Actually, the man wasn't at all interested. He just passed by.

Now I'm going to get something to eat and then concentrate on looking my best tonight. I'm hoping Rich can fix some job for me quickly, in case Roy changes his mind. Feeling as I now do I might so easily give in. And I oughtn't to. While I was talking to Rich's secretary tonight it dawned on me how much I've resented giving up my work. I've never admitted that to myself before. Perhaps that accumulated resentment has made me difficult to live with. Perhaps I'm more to blame for everything than Roy is.

11.15 p.m.
I'm home. According to Tim's ideas of caution I shouldn't be talking now as Roy may be back any minute. But I always

hear the slam of the downstairs front door – and even if I didn't there would be time, after he comes into the flat, to shut the recorder in the basket; I've left it open in readiness. Anyway, I think Tim's a bit dotty about danger – though, quite apart from that, I wouldn't like Roy to know I've taken to talking to a tape-recorder.

Tim was waiting for me at nine-thirty. After a minute or so he said he couldn't concentrate on driving while I was talking or even hear all I was saying, so we drove into a square that was even more dilapidated than ours, and parked.

I suppose I did rather rush at him, trying to give an impression of my whole day. At last he stopped me and said, 'Of course I'm glad about all this from your point of view, but basically it doesn't make any difference.'

I said of course it did. Now that I felt I could trust Roy there couldn't be anything really wrong.

Tim said, 'Well, I hope not. But your personal relations with your husband don't alter the fact that it's at least peculiar for a Member of Parliament to make an assignation with a very odd-looking man and – most surreptitiously – hand something over. Did Mr Mansfield give any reason for letting you go back to the stage?'

'Only that he's out so many evenings. I suppose he thought I might get bored.'

'And bored wives can become curious wives.'

I suddenly felt angry, but I tried not to show it. I said, 'Tim, you've been so wonderfully helpful and kind but, just for the moment, lay off. Don't try to undermine me. And now we must drive to the theatre. At least you approve of my going back to the stage?'

He paused before answering, 'In the long run, of course. But for the moment, well, for God's sake keep on the alert. I *know* you should.'

Poor lad, I suppose the writer in him doesn't want to lose his real-life mystery. He can't possibly *know* anything.

At the theatre he asked if he could wait for me or come back for me. I said I'd rather he didn't as I'd no idea how long I'd be. Actually, I didn't for the moment want any more of Tim. He wished me luck and asked me to let him know how I got on, perhaps I could ring him tomorrow evening. I said not to count on it in case Roy stayed in, but I'd get in touch sooner or later.

There was no one in the foyer except the commissionaire – a new one, who didn't know me. But the nice woman in the box office did. She said, 'He's expecting you,' and gave me a knowing smile – a *nice* knowing smile. Then she telephoned the office and told me he was coming down. Rich always did come down to meet me when I called for him at the theatre. I never liked being alone in the lift, which is perfectly safe but doesn't look it, with its antiquated gate; and I so often pressed the wrong button.

When he opened the gate to let me in, we both said hello and didn't say one word more until we were in the office. I always loved it, with its photographs of dead and gone stars – he's never let anything be changed – and its tall windows where he never draws the curtains. He used to say that was an indication of his blameless life but, actually, only people on neighbouring roof tops could see in.

I said, making conversation, 'How nice to see this room again.'

He put his hands on my shoulders and said, 'Let me have a look at you.'

Only his desk light was on, but it showed him more than I could have wished, for he said, 'More make-up than you used to use and it doesn't suit you. And you're much too thin. What's wrong?'

I said rather loudly, 'Nothing's wrong. Everything's particularly right. Roy says I can act again and he doesn't mind me seeing you. But first tell me about Lyn in New York. How's she done?'

I'd intended to start with that and then lead casually into the possibility of acting again. But I hadn't reckoned on Rich's directness – though I ought to have remembered it.

He said, 'Lyn's done all right but the show's hopeless. It'll close tomorrow.'

'They won't give it a chance?'

'It has none, after yesterday's notices. Anyway, they knew from the previews. Well, there wasn't a penny of my money in it – I never thought it would succeed in New York. Incidentally, it hasn't done all that well here.'

'But it's been running since the autumn.' It opened just after I married Roy, so I've never seen it.

Rich said it'd had a flash-in-the-pan success, which had sold it to New York, mainly as a vehicle for an American male star, 'Who got slated. He won't be pleased to read that a delightful young English actress did all she could to carry the play. That'll please *her*. And I've cabled her that she can take over the part here until the end of the run. Our revered leading lady, who isn't the draw she thinks she is, wants to leave.'

We talked some more about Lyn – she's flying back next week – and then Rich said, 'Now let's talk about you. But first, some champagne.'

It was waiting there. I almost laughed while he opened it. I hadn't set eyes on champagne for months and months, and now, two days running. I said, 'Fancy your remembering.'

'I'm hardly likely to forget the one drink you like – or are you now a more sophisticated drinker?'

'If anything, less.'

'I've been visualising you as a hostess at dazzling political parties.'

'Not Roy's line at all.'

'What *is* his line?'

I took a long gulp of champagne and then said, 'I don't think he's got one yet. He's still quite a new boy, you know, just a backbencher.'

'Of course, of course,' said Rich. 'And when new boys do make a splash it's often a silly one. I'm sure he's a very sound man.'

'By the way, he now thinks you're a very decent chap.'

'Good God, do people still talk about decent chaps?'

'Well, seeing that you've just called him a sound man...'

'But surely you heard my quotation marks?'

Then we began to laugh – I think it was because we were at last at ease with each other. Then Rich said, 'Let's not talk about him or I may say something that annoys you, as I'm not only mad with jealousy but have an inbuilt dislike for men who object to their wives having careers.'

'It wasn't exactly that. We both thought I could do more to help him than I've had the chance to. And now it's *his* suggestion that I should act again.'

'Yes, yes,' said Rich. 'It's obvious that he's a decent chap as well as a sound man. As you've come to me, I take it that you want to work in the theatre. You can pull your own strings in television.'

'I don't want to try that yet. It's the life of the theatre I want – to be there in the evenings.'

Rich said he could understand that. 'You can hardly sit in the House night after night watching your husband sit on a back bench. Well, I can fix you up for the autumn. I don't suppose you'll want to tie yourself up in the evenings when the House goes into the summer recess?'

'I wouldn't mind, really.' Then I rather wished I hadn't said that and added, 'You see, we haven't been able to plan a holiday. Roy has to spend so much time in Midhampton, what with his constituency work and his business.'

Rich thought for a moment, then said, 'Would you be insulted if I suggested that you should understudy Lyn when she takes over here?'

'Would I be ousting someone?'

'Only a good lady who is now covering two parts and would then be covering only one. She's the kind of habitual, unambitious understudy who thinks only in terms of pay packets; I promise you she won't mind. But are you willing to come here as an understudy? You were on the way to becoming a semi-star.'

'Not even a demi-semi-star in the theatre. The last time I played here I was a glorified walk-on. I love the idea of understudying. I'd get the chance to rehearse a big part.'

'That's settled, then,' said Rich. 'We'll leave the salary for the moment. I must find out what the job carries.'

I said, 'Don't pay me more than it's worth.'

'I might pay you more than it's worth, but not more than *you're* worth.'

We went on talking, mainly about the theatre and his autumn plans. I hadn't realised how much I'd missed being 'in the know' about things. Even when I was busy with television he always talked to me about his plans. At last the buzzer rang on his desk, as it always does ten minutes before the fall of the last act curtain. He likes to be in front then and notice audience reactions from different parts of the house. He said, 'Drink up your champagne and then I'll get Soames to drive you home – unless you'll hang on and let me take you out to supper and start feeding you up?'

I said I wanted to be home before Roy got back. I was glad Rich didn't suggest driving with me. Our square looks a little less worse by night than by day, but it's never exactly impressive.

The car was as nostalgic for me as the office had been. Rich so often sent it for me, even when he needed it himself. Soames said how nice it was to see me again and I asked after his wife and children. Then he said I must live a very interesting life now, in 'the world of politics', then added in one of his plunges into weighty courtesy, 'Though, of course, to the stage's loss.' Dear Soames! And dear, dear Rich; he gave me the feeling that, though he still cared for me, there was nothing for me to worry about and I was conferring a great privilege by letting him help me. Why did I never fall in love with him? It's all the more strange because I found everything to do with him, the whole world of the theatre, wildly romantic. Indeed, because of that, I found it romantic to have an affair with him. But I never found *him* romantic. Unfair, that.

I was in such good spirits that I let myself into the house without one thought of possible danger lurking on the stairs. Even when the lights went out, as usual, before I reached the flat, I didn't bother to put on Tim's torch. And after all, if someone's waiting to spring on you, seeing them isn't all that help.

Before I got the tape-recorder out I made myself bread-and-milk. I'm going to take my thinness seriously, and bread-and-milk, with lots of sugar, is the most fattening food I can think of. Luckily, I like it, though I like it best with slabs of plain chocolate; I'll buy some tomorrow. I've been stuffing myself while I've been talking. Now I must put this machine away, before Roy gets back. What a day to look back on! What a happy day!

Oh, God, someone's ringing the downstairs door bell! That's never happened before as late as this. I'm not going down. I shall put off the light and take no notice . . . But suppose it's Roy? Suppose he's forgotten to take his key?

TAPE FIVE

Saturday, June 15th. 10.30 a.m.

Last night! What a shattering ending to my happy day! I decided I must go down in case it was Roy. Then, while I was putting the tape-recorder away, the bell rang again and went on ringing. I couldn't believe Roy would be so insistent, knowing it would take me quite a while to get down. It then struck me that I might be able to see who it was from the window so I flung it open and looked down. I could see the top of a head. It didn't look like Roy, but it was four floors down and the square was very dimly-lit, so I couldn't be sure. I called out, 'Is that you, Roy?' And then the head turned upwards and I saw fair hair, hanging to the shoulders. I felt instantly sure it was the man I'd seen on the bridge in Regent's Park.

He called up that he wanted to see Mr Mansfield and I called down, 'You can't. He's not back yet.'

'Then I'll come in and wait.'

I was furious then, as well as frightened. The arrogance of it! He didn't even *ask* if he could come in. I shouted, 'He won't want to see you as late as this. Anyway, you must make an appointment.'

He said he had one. 'He told me to come.'

I called down, 'Well, I'm sorry, but I'm not letting anyone in at this time of night. Shall I give him a message?'

'I tell you I've got to see him.'

'Then you'll have to wait for him outside.'

I slammed the window down, then put the light off and went back to the window. The man had gone down the steps and was crossing the road. I could see him a little better now and I had no doubt whatever that he was the man I'd seen on the bridge. He went and stood by the railings. Just then a taxi drove into the square. It pulled up, Roy got out, paid it off and came up the steps; but as soon as it was out of sight he went back and crossed the road, then took a package from his briefcase and gave it to the man. They talked together for less than a minute and then the man went off and Roy came towards the house.

At first I thought I'd do nothing. My light was off, he might have noticed that from below and taken it for granted that I'd gone to bed. But suppose the man had mentioned speaking to me? If so, Roy would expect me to refer to it. So I got into my nightdress and dressing gown while he climbed our seventy-two stairs and went to meet him in the hall. I then asked if he'd had a good evening and added quickly, 'Oh, there's just been someone here asking for you.'

He said, 'Yes, I saw him. It was just someone from Midhampton, cadging money. I gave him a few shillings.'

I almost said, 'You did no such thing. You gave him a package you had ready for him.' I stopped myself partly because Tim had warned me against having things out and partly because I couldn't bear to drive Roy into a corner. He's always bad at telling lies, even little social ones, and if he was now so dead set on hiding something from me, well, let him. I felt both angry with him and sorry for him.

He went on to say that he'd decided to go to Midhampton in the morning. 'By the early train and I'll have breakfast on it, so there will be no need for you to get up, if you could throw a few things into my case now. I'll need a dinner-jacket. There's some civic function.'

He got ready for bed while I packed his case and we hardly

spoke at all. He seemed tired and withdrawn, quite unlike the Roy I'd had lunch with, the Roy who'd seemed so much more like his old self. When I got up to see him off this morning he said he'd be back on Monday morning. I said I should be at a rehearsal then and explained, though not in detail, that I'd got a job. He looked surprised for a moment, then said, 'Oh, good. Glad you fixed something so soon. Don't bother about lunch on Monday. I'll go out for it.' And then he smiled, very nicely. For a few seconds there was a sense of contact between us.

But last night had wiped out all yesterday's happiness.

I've rung Tim's number but got no reply; he did say I'd need to ring very early. Anyway, what good would talking to him do? He'd be alarmed about the man in the square, and I'm alarmed, but we both already knew that Roy was in touch with him. All that's really happened is that I've been shaken out of the trust I'd begun to feel in Roy, while he was so kind yesterday; and that's probably as well. Safer.

I don't feel too bad. Perhaps I'm getting used to living in a state of nightmare. And I've got my job to count on. Rich told me to see the play at the five-thirty show today. That'll be a distraction. And now I can get into my bedroom (*my* bedroom, indeed! *My* bedroom now is the size of a prison cell) and concentrate on my clothes.

Sunday, June 16th.   9.30 p.m.

By good luck Tim arrived in the square yesterday just when I was ready to go to the theatre, so I was able to take his taxi and talk to him. He didn't agree with me that the arrival of the man in the square on Friday night indicated nothing new. He said it showed us that the meeting in Regent's Park wasn't just an isolated incident. And he was worried that the man had been so determined to come into the flat. It showed a desperation that might point to a need for drugs. But I simply cannot believe that Roy is handing on drugs.

Tim suggested we might go for a picnic today – not in the taxi; he said he'd borrow a car. I offered to bring the food, but Tim told me his help always leaves him cold food for Sundays and he'd bring that. He said there were various things he wanted to ask me and the picnic would give us a chance for a really private talk. We had a lovely day – but first about the theatre yesterday.

I enjoyed the play though it's not a very good one. I think it's more surprising that it's done quite well here than that it failed in America. I'm not nearly experienced enough for the leading woman's part, but I could certainly 'keep the curtain up' and rehearsals will teach me a lot. I've never before had a chance to play comedy. Lyn will be excellent. She's far cleverer than I am, apart from the fact that she's had more stage experience.

Rich had told me to go round and get a script from the stage manager. He isn't the one I used to know, but he was very pleasant to me and put down far more red carpet than any average understudy would expect. I came home and spent the evening beginning to learn the part. Only as a student have I had to memorise a leading part.

When Tim called for me this morning he came in his taxi. He said calling for me in the sports car he'd borrowed would be too conspicuous. To whom?

We drove to his mews and got out to change into the sports car. I said, 'Let me have another look at that jewel box you live in.' He hesitated for a second before saying, 'All right' – though I can't think why as the room was scrupulously tidy, except for some scattered Sunday papers. It was more glittering and golden than ever, in the bright morning light. It seems ages since I saw it, last Wednesday night. I feel I've lived a lifetime since then.

Tim must have some rich friends. The sports car he'd borrowed was extremely dashing. When I asked him where we were going he said it was a Mystery Trip – and it certainly was to me; I don't know if we drove north, south, east or west. How little I know London and its surroundings. It struck me today that I could, during all the dreary days I've spent on my own this last year, at least have taken some bus trips, done a bit of exploring. I've never even thought of it. I suppose that was part of my ever-increasing inertia.

Tim said he was sorry we had to drive through so many dreary suburbs. They weren't dreary to me – or rather, they were dreary but interesting too. *Everything* was interesting, and it was such bliss to be in an open car. I don't think I ever have before.

At last we were through the suburbs and though we weren't in real country it was pretty and there were some old cottages, a bit too much done-up. And some villages. Tim said they were spoilt but they didn't look bad to me. Then we turned into a lane where there was a notice saying, 'No Through Way'. It was well kept-up at first and there were some done-up cottages, but after the last of these it got narrower and narrower and more overgrown. We had to put up the windows to protect our faces from the hedges – I don't think they did that dashing sports car much good. At last the lane ended in what I took to be a field, but Tim said it had once been the garden of a house that had been burnt down.

He had known the place as a boy, but the house had gone long before that and he knew nothing about it. All that remained now were a few brick foundations, not enough to trace the outline of the house. There was a pond, much overgrown; but quite a lot of the grass was fairly short – Tim said sheep were sometimes grazed here. There were none today, there were no signs of life whatever except birds and insects. And the extraordinary thing was that you couldn't see any houses, whichever way you turned. I suppose hedges and trees blocked the view. There were some elms, a few ancient apple trees, a huge old yew tree and some flowering bushes.

'And,' said Tim, with pride, 'though we're only thirty

miles from London, I've never yet seen another person here.'

It was so sunny that we were glad to settle down on the grass in the shade of the yew tree. Tim had provided a marvellous lunch: cold steak and kidney pie in a blue and white dish, French bread, butter keeping cool in an insulated bag, a cherry cake that was almost all cherries and some tiny Japanese cocktail biscuits I couldn't stop eating. There was champagne wrapped up with cracked ice – when I protested he again mentioned his paperback sale – and a thermos of coffee. While we ate we talked about life in general and I asked him some questions about himself. He wasn't very forthcoming, but I did gather he'd done a number of jobs including acting in reps and bits on television. I suppose he did character work. He could hardly have done anything else, with his diction. I find it puzzling that such a highly-intelligent man, who can write as well as he does, should speak so sloppily. Understanding him is almost like learning a new language, but I've got the knack of it now.

After we finished eating he said, 'Now you talk. Tell me about your whole life and what you know of your husband's. And I'm not just being curious. I might unearth something useful. Now start with yourself – and don't say "There isn't much to tell, really," because there must be one hell of a lot.'

God knows what I told him about myself. He has an extraordinary talent for listening sympathetically and prodding inspiringly. But he didn't manage to prod much about Roy's youth out of me because I know so little about it, except that he had rather a poor education; he went to a private school his father had been to, very old-fashioned and fast running down hill. (I went to a goodish school and, even after father was killed, mother managed to keep me on there.) It's strange how little I know of Roy as a boy and a young man. Yet I wouldn't say that was only due to his reserve; it's more that he doesn't seem interested enough in himself to remember.

At last I said, 'Tim, truly, that's all I can think of about both of us. And I feel positively debauched with self-revelation, and I can't feel that anything I've told you can have helped you much.'

Tim said, 'It has, especially about you. Up to now I've been dealing with – well, a charming stranger. I'd no basis on which I could interpret your behaviour. And you've certainly had me puzzled. I couldn't see how a woman with your looks, past initiative and swift success – oh, you play that down but it was quite considerable – could have accepted these last dreary months. I still don't understand but at least I've got a living, breathing woman to think about; I've got scope for some insight. But about your husband I've got nothing. He's just a pleasantly-mannered, extremely handsome blank to me.'

'You're like Lyn; she calls him a stuffed shirt. She's wrong and you're wrong. How do you suppose he's got where he has? And I'd never have fallen in love with a blank stuffed shirt.'

'And you did, of course, fall in love with him very deeply. Those meetings in Regent's Park——'

'Did I talk much about those?'

'Very little. But enough to give me scope for a little empathy.'

I said I'd never quite known what empathy meant and he explained that, to him, it meant the power of projecting himself into an understanding of other people's feelings. It was the only way he could create character, even the cardboard characters in his thrillers. I said they hadn't seemed cardboard to me.

'Well, I try to make them real, though one mustn't let reality interfere with the story line. About your husband, I didn't mean that he really is a blank, only that he's a blank to me, because you haven't brought him to life for me. I still can't feel you know him very well.'

'I don't as he is now.'

'I wonder if you ever did. I doubt if one ever knows a person one's wildly in love with. It's a sort of intoxication; it clouds the judgement. Your present state's a bit like the morning after a binge; you've got a mental hangover. Listen, I think you should mark time now, give him the benefit of the doubt. I've been so anxious to protect you that I've worked things up too much. Nothing you've told me makes me feel he's basically bad – not bad enough to be a traitor!'

The word horrified me. 'Surely you've never suspected him of that?'

Tim said, 'Well, of course he'd be a traitor if he's involved in espionage. But what seems to me more likely is that he's being blackmailed – possibly blackmailed into supplying someone with drugs. I find that more forgivable than treason.'

I said I wasn't sure I did. 'Some traitors are ideologically convinced they're doing right and one can admire them for the risks they take. But nothing excuses handing on drugs, and to let oneself be blackmailed – well, it's something I can't imagine.'

'I can,' said Tim. 'But then I can imagine almost anything. Hello!'

A very small car was coming down the lane. It drove onto the grass and stopped twenty or so yards away from us. A young man and a young girl got out. I suppose they didn't stare at us any harder than we stared at them – and they smiled, which is more than we did. The girl smiled first, said something which made the young man smile too and then he hurried back to the car.

I whispered to Tim, 'Perhaps they're going.'

'If they don't, we will.' The next minute he said sharply, 'Quick, look down.'

But before I could do so I heard the click of a camera. Then the girl called, 'Hope you don't mind. It's such a thrill, seeing you.'

Tim whispered, 'You've been recognised. Better make the best of it.'

So I called back, 'Nice of you to remember me after so long.'

'Long? We saw you again only last night. I was ever so pleased. It's months since they ran that ad of you in the bath. We always loved it..'

They were moving closer. The camera clicked again. They were rather an appealing couple, both of them short and plump. The girl's legs were far too fat to reveal so much of themselves, yet they were somehow attractive. She now combined a wriggle with a giggle and said, 'Do you really use that soap – I mean, put it on all over you, thick?'

'I did when I made that commercial. I used cakes and cakes of it.'

'I bet you found it dried your skin. Still, they didn't make you put it on your face, did they? – Get a profile of her, Len, like the one where she's lying in the bath.' She turned to Tim. 'Have you been on the telly, too?'

'Never,' said Tim, and started to pack up.

'Here, don't let us drive you away,' said Len. 'We'll be off in a minute.'

'We were going, anyway,' said Tim, quite nicely. 'Have some of these comic biscuits. Oh, not just one, take a handful.'

The girl said she'd take a couple for her little sister, then turned to me. 'Not that she'll believe I've really seen you till the photos get printed. I suppose you wouldn't let me be photographed *with* you?'

'Oh, come off it, Jackie,' said Len.

But I agreed, quite cheerfully. I was enjoying being remembered. Jackie, with a 'Do you mind?', sat down and put her arm through mine. Len said, 'Gorgeous' and clicked the camera, then 'Hold it,' and took another.

Eventually they saw us off, Jackie chattering non-stop about their good luck in turning into the lane by accident. I didn't gather she'd seen me in anything except the bath commercial. Anyway, that was all that counted with her.

As we drove along the lane Tim said, 'Now you see how easy it is to become vulnerable to blackmail.'

'Blackmail? Those two?' The very thought made me laugh.

'No, of course not. Still, I'd as soon there weren't photographs around of you picnicking with your taxi-driver.'

'But I don't mind in the least.'

'You wouldn't mind your husband seeing those snapshots?'

That pulled me up. 'Well, just at the moment, as I'm not supposed to know you well. But normally . . .'

'A man of Mr Mansfield's type would never find it normal. Apart from suspecting you of anything, he'd just think it unsuitable. Oh, don't worry. Those kids were harmless. I'm merely pointing out how the innocent can be liable to blackmail. It's a point in your husband's favour.'

I said that even if the two kids did blackmail me I'd never pay.

'Then you might be foolish because at present, for reasons I won't go into, it might be dangerous to let Mr Mansfield suspect you of anything. But relax now.'

After that, I was surprised that he let us have tea in a village and I noticed that even the waitress looked at me curiously. I'd no idea my bath commercial was extant again.

Tim looked different today. I suppose he'd washed his hair, it seemed fluffier, and he looked less like Simple Simon than a character in a fairy story, say the woodcutter's son. He was extraordinarily nice. I've never known anyone so sympathetic. And he kept surprising me by the things he knew about my feelings. I suppose that was due to what he called 'empathy'.

We got into a few traffic jams on the way home but Tim avoided most of them, by way of backstreets. He says part of the fun of driving a taxi is that you get to know a labyrinth of little streets. He got me home in the early evening, dropping me a short way from our square. Cautious as ever! Being a warm Sunday evening there were more of our neighbours around than usual, children playing, people sitting on their doorsteps. Really, we live in a slum. But I felt a kind of affection for everyone. I think I was a little drunk with air and light and the colour of the country.

After I'd had some supper I made myself study my part for an hour or so, though what I really wanted to do was to settle down to talk to this machine. It's becoming a compulsion. I think some people feel that way about their diaries. I couldn't possibly write one. I mean I couldn't be natural with one. Even when writing a letter I have to plan the words ahead. But I sure can talk. . . .

I've been looking out of the window. Although it's dark now there are still people on their doorsteps or their balconies, or leaning out of top windows. This is the first time it's occurred to me that our slum's romantic. No doubt it's a question of my mood. I keep going back over the day, our lunch under the yew tree; fat, funny Jackie and Len. And Tim's extreme kindness. It has a quality of gentleness, almost sweetness – though I don't for one moment think he's queer. He hasn't mentioned any girls in his life, but then he's concentrating on drawing me out. One particularly nice thing was that he showed sympathy for Roy, seemed – about blackmail – to be on his side. I'll try to be, too. I'll remember that moment on Friday when he held out his hand and said he was sorry for everything. I'll have faith—— There's the telephone.

I'm back, and shaking with rage. That was Rich on the telephone. He began by saying, 'Does the sound man permit your manager to ring you up at home?'

I said it might be tactful to keep the home calls to a minimum, but Roy wasn't in. 'So you can go ahead and I'm happy to hear from you.'

He wanted to know how I'd got on with his stage manager, Bart Holland, who takes the understudy rehearsals. He'd told Rich he was much impressed by me – but that was probably Rich dropping a little tactful oil in the machine. Then he informed me Lyn will be flying home tomorrow. And then, after a general gossip, he asked me if I would lunch with him after the morning rehearsal. He added nicely, 'Don't feel you have to, if it will upset Roy.' I was about to say I'd give Roy a little while to get used to my being back in the theatre before I went out with Rich, when he went on, 'He must be pleased with his publicity today. He made two front pages.'

I said blankly, 'What?'

'Haven't you seen any Sunday papers?'

'They hadn't arrived when I went out this morning and they weren't on the steps when I came back. I suppose someone swiped them. Why, was Roy in them?'

'He was with his dear friends, the Slepes. They've decided to give England another chance.'

'You mean they're back?'

'The photographs were taken yesterday, on the terrace at Slepe. And there's a striking article by Cyprian in *The Observer* – or is it *The Sunday Times?* – the gist being that they left England because they couldn't stand living here any longer, but they've found every country they went to far worse, so they've come home to fight, well, practically everything. The strange thing is that Cyprian's quite convincing. I've always loathed him, but I now feel he may be sincere.'

I said brightly, 'Well, I shall hear all about it when Roy gets back. About tomorrow, yes, I'd love to have lunch with you. And thank you for everything.' I longed to get off the telephone before I gave away how I was feeling about Roy.

'I'll pick you up after rehearsal,' said Rich. 'Goodnight, my dear.'

It's as well that Roy's not coming back tonight – or is it? Perhaps it would be a good thing if I let him know my feelings at this moment. There's not one iota of love in them, nothing but blazing rage. Not to tell me the Slepes were back and he was off to join them! Leaving me to find it out from the Sunday papers! My God, they're hogs for publicity – and how do they manage to get it? Why does anyone want to read about them?

How bloody *stupid* of him not to tell me! I suppose he funked it. Now I know why he said I could work again. He thought it would keep me occupied and leave him free to spend all his time with his dear patrons.

Are they connected with his handing packets to the awful man with dyed hair? I can't think how. One glorious ironic note: if the Slepes *are* involved with his recent mysterious behaviour he's certainly no spy – unless Hitler and Mussolini ride again. Anything less likely than a tie-up between the dear Fascist Slepes and Red Russia I can't imagine.

Shall I ring Tim? He'd be relieved to know Roy can't be involved in espionage. But now I come to think of it, he can make that deduction himself. He must already have seen the Sunday papers, they were scattered around in his sitting-room this morning; that would account for his hesitation about inviting me in. As I didn't refer to them, he'd take it for granted I hadn't seen them and lay off mentioning them in case it spoilt my day. I won't ring him. I won't burden him with my rage.

Perhaps rage is better than the desperate anxiety I've so often felt these last days. In a way, it's stopped me from *minding* so much about Roy. If I once stop caring for him perhaps I shan't mind if he's a blackmailed drug-peddler *and* a spy. All I shall care about is extricating myself from him. Have I got to that stage yet?

TAPE SIX

Monday, June 17th. 9 p.m.

Rehearsal this morning: everyone was nice to me, particularly the woman who's relinquishing her job to me – that is, just her job of understudying the lead; she's still covering her other part. She says she'll now be able to leave in time to catch an earlier train home. Not having understudied before I hadn't realised you have to stay in the theatre until the last entrance of anyone you're understudying. (If they then drop dead on stage, that's that.)

Bart Holland stopped strewing roses today and gave me some valuable criticism. He says that as nearly all my experience has been on television, I don't yet know how to *project* in the theatre. One merely has to *be* on television, but that kind of performance would barely reach the front rows in a theatre. That's why many brilliant television performers are disappointing on the stage – and why some stage stars seem unreal on television, though I gather it's easier to tone yourself down than tone yourself up. So Bart wants me to work on this from the beginning. He says that if I over-act, even shout, it doesn't matter. He can easily correct that. What I mustn't do is to settle for giving a television performance – which, on the stage, will be a mere indication of a performance.

Of course I'm being given far more help than most understudies are given. They're usually expected, more or less, to copy the performance of the principal they're understudying, so that they won't be a nuisance to the rest of the cast when they have to play. Bart says Rich asked him to direct me as if I were creating a part, not copying it, so that it'll help me in the future. I apologised for giving so much trouble, but Bart said it was a blessed change.

Just this one rehearsal has brought back all my longing to act, especially in the theatre. I was so happy – and so surprised – to do well in television that it almost made me forget it was my longing for the *theatre* that brought me from Midhampton, and made me risk every penny I had in keeping myself while I trained. Bart said—— I want to talk more about this, but there's so much of this extraordinary day I need to record first.

When I woke up this morning I'd stopped being furious with Roy. I suppose I still felt resentful, but I was mainly conscious of a determination to think about him as little as possible and, above all, not to let him have any effect on my work at rehearsal. It was as if I pulled a mental shutter down against him. And it worked; otherwise I shouldn't have done so well – that is, Rich said I did. He came in for a few minutes without letting me see him. And though he agrees with Bart that I'm not projecting enough, he says that will come.

For lunch we went to a new restaurant, suddenly fashionable, and there were so many people who remembered me that I accused Rich of planting them there, to encourage me. He admitted to scattering a few hints that I'd be lunching with him there and that I was coming back to the theatre. People came and talked and were *so* nice. And they were polite about Roy, whom they'd seen in the Sunday papers, and gave the impression of thinking that being the wife of a Member of Parliament was extremely important. But someone said, 'Still, I bet you've got tired of opening bazaars and garden fêtes.' Not one bazaar or garden fête have I been asked to open.

We were just settling down to eat when Rich looked up and said, 'Good God, there's Celina Slepe!' She was standing in the doorway, gazing around and a great many people were gazing back at her – and no wonder. I hadn't realised from photographs quite how tall and thin she is, and her height was accentuated by a tall hat with even taller feathers. She was aflutter with scarves, draperies and swirling fringes and loaded with barbaric jewellery. And the odd thing was that though her get-up was quite like that of some of the 'with it' young, she didn't look 'with it'. She looked eccentric in a long-outdated way. Rich said, 'She's a pure Aubrey Beardsley,' and he meant the 'pure' literally, for her face isn't vicious or decadent. It has a childlike vacuity – as I realised when she swooped down on our table screaming, a breathy child-like scream, 'Rich! How marvellous! Did you see us in the papers yesterday? Didn't we look lovely?'

She didn't take the slightest notice of me. Rich, having got up and taken the hand she held out – there seemed to be more rings than hand – said, 'Nan, have you met Celina Slepe? This is Nan Sheldon, Celina – Mrs Roy Mansfield.'

She looked at me then all right. In fact, she stared, blankly. Then she said, without the flicker of a smile, 'Do you mean you're Roy's wife? I couldn't be more surprised. Are you the one who appeared nude on television?'

I said, 'Well, as far as I know I'm the only wife he has. And I wasn't quite nude on television. They let me keep a little unseen bikini.'

'How horrid! Bikinis are so vulgar, aren't they? Of course I never saw you myself – I don't watch television. But Cyprian does. How stupid of him to give me the wrong impression of you. She's lovely, isn't she, Rich? I must paint her.' She turned to me, still without the flicker of a smile. 'Come to Slepe next weekend, with Roy.'

I said, 'Sorry. I shan't be free.'

'Then the next weekend.'

'I shan't be free then, either.'

. 'Oh, dear, I've offended you. Rich, tell her it's just my way and I can't help it.'

Rich said, 'That's perfectly true. But you can help spoiling our lunch. I'm tired of standing up.'

'Then sit down. I'll join you.' She looked vaguely round for a chair.

A hovering waiter approached. Rich shook his head at him. 'No, Celina. We don't want you to join us. We want you to go away.'

'But I must make her understand.' At last she smiled at me, a tentative smile, like that of an uncertain child. 'It's all Cyprian's fault. He's hopeless at describing women – not that he's a queer; I often wish he were, they're so nice. And I'm not a Les – truly. I just want to paint you. *Do* come to Slepe.'

I shook my head and said, 'Sorry. Can't be done.'

'Oh, dear! I must talk to Roy.' She looked around, piteously, as if for help. Then her expression brightened. 'Oh, there are the people I'm lunching with. Darlings!' She screamed it across the restaurant, but again it only came out as a breathy wail. The next minute she was moving to join her friends, somehow suggesting a giraffe out of control.

I said to Rich, 'It's just not true. None of that could possibly have happened.'

'It did, and I've known her far worse. I saw quite a lot of her at one time when she had an idea she could act. You see, she's so extraordinary that I felt it worth while to have some patience with her. She just might have turned out to have genius.'

'But she hadn't?'

'Not for acting. She was like a survival from some film made long before she was born. I did think her paintings had something, but she's never got anywhere with them. They're mainly vague swirls of rather beautiful colour, apparently meaningless and lacking the authority really good abstracts have. You should get it into your head, Nan, that she can't help being what she is. She can't even help her rudeness. She's incapable of thinking before she speaks. In some ways she's childish – oh, not feeble-minded, just not fully mature.'

'I'm beginning to believe what Roy says about never having had an affair with her.'

'I'd find it far more difficult to believe that he ever had. She's simply not old enough for it, mentally. She did once tell me, with her usual lack of inhibitions, that she'd "tried" sex. She said it didn't work for her and she had an idea that she wasn't rightly made – whatever that meant. I didn't enquire in case she told me.'

I asked if her brother had the same kind of immaturity.

'Oh, no. Cyprian's abnormally *old*. At thirty-seven he's at least two years older than God. If he's not queer – and I think she's right about that – it's because he outgrew such trivialities as sex before he was born. I don't know him as well as I know her, but I did once visit them at Slepe and I should say that, while she's basically silly, he's basically bad. You should, by the way, accept her invitation.'

I looked at him in astonishment. 'After her outrageous rudeness?'

'I've told you, that's meaningless. And apart from the fact that you'd find Slepe fascinating, don't you want to know two people who are obviously going to be important to your husband's career? Still, that's not my business. You're looking worried. Let's talk of something else.'

The reason I was looking worried was that I'd suddenly remembered how furious I was with Roy. It had come back to me with a rush. And this time I didn't intend to bottle it up.

But something astonishing happened when I got back to the flat. Roy was there and, as our bi-weekly cleaning lady was pottering around, he'd asked her to make him some tea.

As I went into the sitting-room he said, 'Oh, good! Ask Mrs Thing for another cup and some more hot water. And tell me how your rehearsal went.'

I closed the door behind me and said, reasonably quietly, 'Why didn't you tell me you were going to spend the weekend with the Slepes?'

'Because I didn't know I was going to until I got to the hotel on Saturday morning and found them there. The Hall isn't opened yet. We just went there to be photographed. I didn't even know they were going to be back in England.'

No doubt he saw the disbelief in my eyes for he went on, 'Yes, I suppose it sounds unlikely but it's true. Oh, I knew they were planning to return, but no dates were fixed. In fact, the last time I saw them they still weren't sure they'd come.'

'When *was* the last time you saw them?'

He said it was about a month ago, when he went to the Continent on business for his firm. He hadn't told me about the meeting because there was no point in upsetting me until their plans were more definite. 'I know that, very naturally, you've always resented the idea of them. But things will be different now. After seeing you at lunch, Celina thinks you're wonderful and says will you please, please come to Slepe with me next weekend? I promised to telephone her back and say you would.'

'Well, you can telephone her back and say I bloody well won't. I think you must be out of your mind.'

'Don't shout,' said Roy. 'Mrs Thing's still here.'

I heard the front door slam. 'She's gone now so I can shout as much as I like. Not that I really want to. It's all right, Roy. I know how important the Slepes are to you and I'll be civil to them if I happen to meet them. But I won't visit them just because that unbelievable woman snaps her fingers at me. Now, I'll make a fresh pot of tea and take it to my cell.'

'Before you go, will you listen to me?'

It was the strangest thing. There was something different about his voice, his expression, his whole personality; a sincerity which made me realise how insincere he's been for weeks now. I sat down and said, 'Right. Go ahead.'

I'm still a bit bewildered by what he said. Some of it links with what he hinted at on our happy day last Friday. He told me now that he'd begun to fear he had no future in politics, that he'd let the Slepes boost him into a position he couldn't sustain. He's still uncertain, but now they are back and determined to help him, he wants to give himself another chance. But he won't unless I support him, by which he means that I must be on friendly terms with the Slepes. He'd feared that was impossible. It's been on his mind for weeks. I think he has known, for certain, that they were coming back. I don't think he was honest about that, and quite a few things he said don't really make sense – though I was careful never to catch him out. I'd say they've been far more resentful about me than I've been about them, and have been determined to have nothing to do with me. Now, it appears, Celina – God damn her impertinence – thinks I shall be 'a definite asset'.

One thing I feel sure of: it's something more than a loss of confidence in himself that has undermined him. There's something he hasn't told me, but I believe that, this afternoon, he was being basically sincere and he was asking me for help – he never has before. I said I'd go with him to the Slepes.

He then wanted to know if I had the right clothes. I've bought no evening dresses since we married and what I have aren't very exciting, so I thought I might borrow something from the theatre wardrobe.

'The wardrobe?' said Roy, with the utmost horror, making it sound like a second-hand clothes shop. 'Can't you buy some new dresses?'

'Only at great expense – and, anyway, I haven't the time.

Don't worry. I'll do you credit.'

·'From now on you must spend more money on yourself. And we ought to get a better flat.'

Very strange. For months he's given me the impression that we're short of money. Now we're suddenly rolling.

He's dining with the Slepes to-night, at the Ritz, where they're staying——

There's the telephone.

Tuesday, June 18th.   10 p.m.

When I broke off last night it was Lyn on the telephone, back from New York already. I lunched with her today, after rehearsal.

This morning I took Tim's taxi to drive to the theatre and had the chance to tell him about the weekend at Slepe ahead of me. He said I must keep my eyes open though he didn't see how Roy's handing over packages could be linked with the Slepes. I said I didn't either and, anyway, I was going to try to forget about it for the present.

'Okay, if you say so,' said Tim. 'Though shutting your eyes to it won't mean it didn't happen. Still, what worries me more now is that you may pour the whole story out to your friend Lyn.'

'I won't. I'd hate her to know that I suspect Roy.'

Actually, I found I had no desire to tell her. There was so much more to talk about: her time in America, the play's failure, her taking over the part in London the week after next, my understudying her. She said everyone is saying I shall go back to Rich, 'everyone' being two people she's spoken to on the telephone and she admitted she'd put the idea into their heads. We barely mentioned Roy.

We lunched in her ancient flat which I love so dearly. It's almost old enough to have a preservation order on it, as an example of early flat architecture. The dining-room is in the hall under a circular skylight which is, as it always was, filthy. I paid a nostalgic visit to my old bedroom – pitch black, looking onto a deep well. I still find the sitting-room attractive, with its sloping walls and dormer windows. I'd forgotten how loud the roar of the traffic from Holborn is. I even found that attractive. What fun Lyn and I had together!

After lunch I met Rich in the theatre wardrobe. He'd already sorted out some possibilities for me to borrow. One reason for his success is his grasp of the detail of his productions, and he has a fantastic memory. He had the wardrobe mistress – she's new since my days – hunting for accessories such as bags and scarves that he hadn't seen for months. He even remembers all *my* clothes and said one of my evening dresses which he particularly liked was quite good enough for Friday night dinner, but I must have something gaudier for Saturday and black lace for Sunday. I told him I'd never stayed at a great country house – or any country house, for that matter – and I'd an idea that grand weekends were a thing of the past. I didn't want to overdress. He said, 'You *can't* overdress for Slepe. Celina will look like the Queen of Sheba and Cyprian will sport a white tie, or knee-breeches, or both.'

I shall look quite up to Queen of Sheba standards in the Saturday night dress. It was imported for some choosy foreign star, who then declined to wear it. She said it would swamp her. Rich says it won't swamp me – which is a compliment to my looks which I can't feel they deserve, though I am looking better. Of course, I'm not any fatter yet but, as Rich pointed out, I'm carrying my head better. He says the haggard look I had last week was largely mental. Rich is doing wonders for my self-confidence. I find it extraordinarily reassuring to be with a man with whom I was once on such complete terms of intimacy and to feel sure he still has so much affection for me. I am always completely at ease with him.

Roy's dining with the Slepes again tonight – there's the downstairs front door slamming. He's back! Into the basket with this tape-recorder.

TAPE SEVEN

Monday, June 24th. 4.00 p.m.

It's absurd how nervous I feel because I'm officially starting as an understudy tonight. Nothing's less likely than that I should have to play, particularly as Bart admits I haven't had enough rehearsals to be safe and, if some sudden emergency occurred, he'd probably call on the nice woman who's been covering the part from the beginning of the run and has played several times. I'm glad to say she and I are sharing a dressing-room. She's good company.

From now on I shall only get one run-through a week. But Lyn starts rehearsing tomorrow, to take over the part, and I can learn a lot by watching her.

Roy's out, helping the Slepes to flat-hunt, so I can set about describing the Hall. It's strange that, though I've lived within five miles of it most of my life, I've never until this weekend set eyes on it. Of course it's not open to the public *ever* and you can't see it from any road as it's hidden by woods and, in one place, by what looks like a ruined castle; actually it's a fake, built in the eighteenth century to make a picturesque view from the Hall. Even when you're through the massive iron gates – our taxi-driver had to open them (there was no car waiting for us at Midhampton station) – you have to drive a long way before you see the Hall.

It wasn't in the least like what I expected. There are postcards of it on sale in Midhampton, so I suppose I must have confused the ruin with the Hall in my memory as I was expecting something far more romantic. On a first glance I thought the house ugly and forbidding. Across the whole of the front are thick pillars, going right up to the roof and supporting an overpowering portico. On one side I could see two rows of tall, narrow windows on the ground floor and first floor, and above the top row was a stone parapet behind which you could just see the tops of small windows. I took these to belong to servants' rooms (but I was wrong!) Everywhere there was dark, dirty-looking stone; no colour anywhere except the surrounding grass and that looked parched. It was late afternoon, sunless, which added to the general impression of gloom; but next day I walked round the Hall on a sparkling morning and I'm not sure it didn't look even more gloomy by contrast with the sunlight.

The taxi-driver helped us to carry our cases up the steps to the front double doors – enormously high and firmly closed. Roy pulled a bell which clanged a long way off. The taxi man said, 'Want me to stay and see if you get in? I thought they were still away.' Roy said no and paid the man off. We stood there waiting. I suggested Roy should ring again but he said, 'Not yet. It's a long walk from the kitchen quarters.' At last we heard footsteps and then bolts were drawn back and the doors were opened by a handsome, elderly butler; with him, believe it or not, were two footmen in livery. One, who was very red in the face, looked like a farm boy. The other was good-looking and extremely correct – like a footman in a play. For a second I thought I knew his face but I couldn't place him, and he showed no sign of recognising me.

I had expected to be shown in to a group of guests having an elegant afternoon tea. There was no one at all in the vast hall and, as the light only came in from the windows under the deep portico, there was barely enough of it for us to see our way to the staircase. The butler said to the footmen, 'The red and gold bedrooms,' then, to me, 'Dinner will be at eight.

Will there be anything more, madam?' It seemed an odd thing to say as there hadn't yet been anything.

We followed the footmen up the wide but quite steep stone staircase which led to a gallery, onto which several tall doors stood open. (Later I discovered there was a ballroom and a picture gallery on that floor.) We went up higher and found our bedrooms were two of the rooms with windows behind the stone parapet. The correct-looking footman said, 'Madam will prefer the gold room.' I wondered why – until I saw the red room.

Both rooms were long, narrow and very dark because of the parapet. The walls of 'the gold room' were entirely covered with a swirling design in shades of yellow which I guessed – from what Rich had told me – must have been painted by Celina. The red room was all swirling reds. It looked like a cell in hell. There were narrow brass bedsteads, not new, fashionable now but old and dilapidated, and marble-topped washstands with china ewers, basins and chamber pots. It had just flashed through my mind that the rooms were a joke that was being played on us when the correct-looking footman said, 'Let me show you the bathroom.'

It was next door to my room, another narrow slice, the bath apparently decorated by Celina. The footman said, 'Unfortunately the hot water no longer comes up, but I'll bring you some at once.'

As soon as both footmen had gone I looked blankly at Roy who looked back equally blankly. Then he said he simply didn't understand it; he'd always had a grand, if uncomfortable, bedroom on previous visits. Perhaps the house was unusually full.

He seemed so embarrassed that I felt sorry for him and decided to make the best of things. So I said, 'Well, it's all very interesting and Celina's quite a painter.' We were in the red room then and I went round looking at the walls, not that I could see much of them even though I'd snapped the light on, as there was only one bulb in the ceiling and that was partly obscured by red beads. Then we heard heavy footsteps and the younger footman, out of breath and even redder in the face, hurried in holding out a salver with a letter on it. He said, 'For the mister,' and dashed away as soon as Roy had picked up the letter.

Roy opened the envelope and said, 'It's a note from Cyprian: "No doubt your wife will wish to rest after her journey. Please join us in the library for an urgent discussion." I suppose I'd better go. I *am* sorry about all this.'

I told him not to worry and I should be quite glad of a rest. What I really meant to do was to unpack for both of us and then do a bit of exploring; but before I was ready to, the correct-looking footman came back with a copper jug of hot water which he was taking to the bathroom. I saw him through my open door – my room was very airless and I hadn't been able to get my window open; so I asked him to try. He managed to budge the sash about three inches and while he was wrestling with it I had a good look at him and suddenly placed him. I said, 'Dick Stanton!' And then he swung round saying how nice it was of me to remember him. Then we were well away on a conversation.

He'd been in two episodes of my last television series, playing a small part extremely well. He was quick to let me know that he wasn't down and out; he had a television play lined up. But between jobs he and some of his friends often did domestic work, usually in London, but this time his agency had been asked to supply a country-house staff for the weekend, and he'd thought it would be fun. The housemaid and the parlour-maid were out-of-work actresses and the butler was an old actor who had specialised in butlers but had, of course, no idea of a real butler's work. The only professional servant in the group was the cook, who kept threatening to walk out.

'We keep jollying her into staying,' said Dick who, by now,

was sitting beside me on the bed, 'but I doubt if Tom – he's the other footman – will stay the course. He's a farm boy whose mother does some cleaning here and he thinks he's got into a madhouse – as, indeed, he has.'

The Slepes have no idea what kind of servants they've got. Celina has only once entered the kitchen, when she told the cook to serve a swan for Saturday's dinner. The cook said she had never cooked a swan and, anyway, hadn't got one to cook. 'Miss Slepe said she could get one off the lake, and then walked away. Naturally, the cook was outraged, but then Tom told her there were no swans on the lake and there now wasn't really any lake; it was mainly mud. Honestly, Nan, are the Slepes round the bend? I mean, really?'

I said I thought they were merely eccentric egoists, trying to live in the past.

'But it's not a past they can possibly remember,' said Dick. 'The days of swans for dinner and fully-staffed country houses were before they were born.'

Still wondering why Roy and I had been given such awful bedrooms, I asked how many other weekend guests there were. Dick said only one – 'Some kind of foreign count. I didn't get his name, it's probably Dracula. He's got what's called "the King's Room". In this whole huge house there are only five good bedrooms. They're on the floor below, at the back of the house. Celina and Cyprian have one each. Celina has one as a studio and Cyprian has one as a study. That only leaves one proper guest room, which the Count has.'

I gathered that the rest of the first floor was taken up with the picture gallery – 'without any paintings except Celina's' – and the ballroom. Down below is the dining-room, a drawing-room and a library 'with hardly any books,' and the central hall. The reason why the hall is so dark is that it's supposed to be lit by a glass roof, which has had to be boarded over for safety. According to Dick, the whole house is pretty well falling to pieces.

The servants' bedrooms are in the basement. 'We nearly walked out on sight of them, but in some ways they're better than these rooms. The windows are up near the ceilings and you can just see the sky if you jump. Up here the windows are so low that only your feet can see out and all they can see is the parapet.'

We kept laughing. I told Dick I'd come expecting to move for the first time in my life in high society. Dick said whatever it had once been, it was now high and dry society. He felt sure the Slepes must be broke. 'Luckily we got paid in advance by the agency, but whether the agency gets its money back is another matter.'

He's picked up quite a lot of information from Tom. 'He's quite bright, once he's not expected to what he calls "play act" a footman. There are local tradesmen's bills outstanding from when the Slepes were last in England. They're having to pay cash for what's coming into the house now.'

How on earth were the Slepes – as I now saw them – going to help Roy's career? And did he know they are in such a bad way financially? That is, if they really are; they've been talking about taking an expensive London flat. I was sure, anyway, that he wouldn't approve of my gossiping about them. And he wouldn't think it amusing that the staff was mainly composed of out-of-work stage people. So I told Dick I wasn't going to mention this.

'Quite right,' said Dick. 'We've got to do our best to behave like real servants. And don't you go catching my eye at dinner tonight.'

We'd kept the door open and just then we heard footsteps in the passage (uncarpeted). Dick went out hastily, then returned to say it was only Jennifer and Sylvia, the 'parlour-maid' and 'housemaid'. They'd ostensibly come up to turn down the beds, but they were hoping to get a word with me. So of course I asked them in.

They were young and pretty and *so* nice. We did a lot more gossiping and laughing. I felt guilty about my hosts, but I must say I enjoyed myself. The girls wanted to know if I could give them any hints about behaviour, especially Jennifer, who was going to help Dick serve dinner. 'Mr Francis will just hover in the background. He doesn't know a thing about serving.'

'Still, he looks lovely,' said Sylvia. 'Every inch a butler.'

We pooled all we knew about such things as serving over the left shoulder but, actually, they all knew more than I did as they'd often helped at London dinner parties. 'It's just that this is such a formal occasion,' said Jennifer, 'with lots of courses. It's going to be a bit like one of those nightmares where you have to play a part without knowing any of your lines.'

Dick said Mr Francis remembered four speeches he'd used when playing butlers: 'Very good, sir.' 'Will there be anything more, madam?' 'Thank *you*, sir,' and 'I will endeavour to ascertain, my lord.'

Soon a gong boomed through the house. Dick said it was the dressing gong; Mr Francis had been told to ring it at seven. Then they all went downstairs, expecting Roy to come up and dress, which he shortly did.

I was determined to make no further comments on the Slepes or their extraordinary house, so I just said brightly, 'Everything going well?'

He said, 'Er, yes, but it's all a little complicated. Nothing I can talk about as yet.'

Then we went into our separate cells to dress.

At a quarter to eight we went downstairs together. There were enough lights on in the hall now to show up the general dilapidation. Some of the black and white squares of the marble floor were missing. But the Slepes looked truly splendid. Celina was in sea-green chiffon, swathed almost like a mummy, with ropes and ropes of beads and a Cleopatra-like head dress. Cyprian was in grey-and-silver brocade, a sort of strictly-tailored dressing-gown, a froth of ruffles at his throat. Like Celina, he's enormously tall and he's even fairer than she is. In fact, he's almost an albino, except that his eyes are bright blue. Like his sister's, his head is too small for his body and he, too, has exquisite features. But there's one great difference between their looks: whereas Celina's face has an innocuous prettiness, Cyprian's expression is arrogant. And their personalities are very different. Celina babbles away like a child. Cyprian speaks very deliberately. And there's some warmth about Celina's silliness. Cyprian appears to be anything but silly, and quite icily cold. He gave me one appraising blue glance as we shook hands and I instantly felt he disliked me (and how right I was!).

Standing with them was a short, heavy old man with thick white hair and eyebrows, very dark eyes and a heavily-lined, aristocratic face. This was the Count and neither then, nor later, did I manage to make out his name; it sounded like a collection of consonants. Anyway, he was always addressed as 'Count'. He spoke excellent English but with a strong accent. Actually, I didn't hear him say very much that first night as, the minute introductions were over, Cyprian began to hold forth and went on almost non-stop throughout dinner – which was in a vast dining-room, but on a small table which seemed unsuited to the room. The only light was from candles on the table and a few on the sideboard, which was so far away that the 'butler' and his helpers were little more than faceless shadows to me, except when Dick and Jennifer were actually handing dishes. They did this very well, right through the six courses (which were excellently cooked). Half way through the meal I saw poor old Mr Francis sit down, which was hardly butlerish behaviour, but I'm pretty sure the Slepes didn't notice. Cyprian was too busy talking and Celina too busy listening, as if entranced.

I have never in my life heard anyone talk as Cyprian did. He spoke of politics, religion, the arts, history, almost every country in the world, the past, the present and the future. Much of what he said was, I'm sure, brilliant but there came a time when I could no longer take in any more. It wasn't really conversation at all. It was a lecture, delivered in a voice that was sometimes silky but, more often, bitingly sarcastic. Whenever he paused to eat – and he didn't eat much – Celina said something like, 'How true! How right you are, Cyprian.' The rest of us made occasional attempts to speak and when the Count spoke Cyprian listened with reasonable civility, but he did not appear to *hear* Roy or me, unless we asked some question he felt like answering and then he was off on another non-stop monologue.

During one short respite, when Cyprian was eating, drinking, or helping himself to something Dick handed, I made the mistake of asking if the public were ever admitted to see the house. It was idiotic of me because I already knew that they weren't, and that the Slepes – according to Roy – disapproved of showing country houses to what Cyprian called 'oafs'. He was down on me instantly, saying that if he couldn't afford to keep Slepe sacrosanct he would rather leave it to moulder into decay. He then treated us to a great set-piece about the walls crumbling, giant weeds obscuring the broken windows, the roof and then the staircase falling, the surrounding park becoming an impenetrable wilderness.

'That would have beauty and dignity,' he said.

'Oh, no, no, no,' wailed Celina, like a child repudiating a sad story.

'Don't worry, my dear,' said Cyprian, sounding almost kind. 'It won't happen. Instead, the great days will soon come again.'

I began to wonder if he was slightly mad and I wondered it even more next day, when I'd seen more of the house and realised how far gone it is already. But surely a madman couldn't talk as brilliantly as Cyprian does? Some of what he said was over my head, but I'm sure it *was* brilliant.

At the end of dinner he quite obviously signalled to Celina that she should take me away and, when we rose, he said, 'My dear, will you entertain Mrs Mansfield for the rest of the evening? The Count, Roy and I have things to discuss which would be of no interest to either of you.'

So we dim-wits were banished to our female chatter – not that I minded; I wasn't exactly looking forward to being alone with Celina but I was certainly looking forward to getting away from Cyprian. For one thing, every time he looked at me I felt he hated me.

As we went towards the door Celina said to the butler, 'We'll have coffee in my studio.' Mr Francis (on his feet again now) was able to answer, 'Very good, madam,' most impressively.

We trailed through the hall and up the wide staircase, then along a passage to the back of the house. At last Celina flung open the double-doors of a very large room dimly lit by a candelabra; only a few of the electric bulbs in the candelabra were working. I took in three tall uncurtained windows and a great many unframed canvases standing on the floor. A few framed ones were hung on the green-painted panelling. There was very little furniture except a huge circular divan in the middle of the room, piled with cushions. Celina said, 'Do sit down – or rather, lie down. It's much more comfortable.'

She then flung herself down among the cushions. I sat, rather gingerly, on the edge of the divan and looked around at what were obviously Celina's paintings. They were all vague, swirling shapes, but paler than the walls of our bedrooms and difficult to make out in the dim light.

Celina said, 'Don't look at them now, they need daylight. I'm going to start painting you tomorrow. I did think you should be all grey and white and flesh colour, but now I think that would be too nebulous. I may have to put in one feature – that's my latest style – but I don't know which feature. I'll decide tomorrow. Tell me what you think of Cyprian. Isn't he astonishing?'

I said I certainly thought he was astonishingly clever.

'Oh, that, of course – much too clever for me to understand. But he's more than clever; he's dynamic and I can understand that. He's going to save the whole world by some marvellous scheme. Oh, dear, he told me not to mention that to you. But I haven't given anything away, really, because I've no idea what the scheme is. I only know that Roy and the Count are going to help him – and other people later on. Roy's wonderful, isn't he? I was once in love with him and he quite liked me, but it was all before he knew you so you won't mind, will you?'

I said I didn't mind at all.

'And you won't mind if I go on being in love with him – in a distant sort of way? I mean, he's nice to think about. Though I'd just as soon think about you. It's got nothing to do with sex.'

Then Dick brought the coffee in. He looked round for a table to put the tray on, but there was none to be seen. Celina patted the divan and said, 'Put it here and I must try not to roll on it.'

Dick poured the coffee out, then said, 'Will that be all, madam?' with a dead straight face. Celina, still flat on her back, stared up at him for at least a minute before answering, 'Yes, yes. You may go.' As soon as he'd closed the door behind him she said to me, 'Nice, isn't he? Someone to think about.' So presumably Dick has now joined Roy and me in her fantasies.

I wondered how I could get through the evening with her, but I soon found I only had to listen. Away from Cyprian she became as compulsive a talker as he is, but whereas his conversation is brilliant and incisive, hers is vague and at times almost nonsensical – but never quite nonsensical and sometimes she says something illuminating.

For instance——

TAPE EIGHT

Tuesday, June 25th. 2.00 p.m.

I broke off yesterday because Roy came home earlier than I had expected. I was so absorbed in remembering Slepe that he was in the flat before I heard him. During the daytime there's no slam of the downstairs door to alert me and, though I did hear the front door closing, I must still have been talking when he was inside the hall. I went out to greet him and said brightly, 'Did you hear me rehearsing my part?'

He said, 'Yes, I guessed that's what you were doing.'

I doubt if there was time for him to hear any actual words and presumably I had a lucky escape. But I must be more careful in future.

When I broke off yesterday I'd just said, 'For instance'. Now I can't remember how I meant to go on. That evening in Celina's studio is now just a blur of talk in my memory, with her rolling about on the huge divan, and again and again narrowly missing the coffee tray. It was nearly midnight before she said we must go to bed, so that she would be fresh to paint me in the morning. She asked me if I would like to get up at dawn – 'I see you as a dawn person.' I said I thought ten o'clock would be early enough. Mercifully, she didn't argue, just said, 'All right. I expect someone will bring you breakfast. Cyprian and I never get up for it.'

My bedroom was hot and airless and the bed had two cleverly placed broken springs. I lay awake until after two, when I heard Roy come up to bed. I was wakened at nine when Jennifer brought me quite a good breakfast. She sat and talked to me while I ate it. I learned from her that Roy was breakfasting in Cyprian's bedroom. 'Dick says Mr Slepe's wearing a kaftan and a turban.' The 'servants' had slept worse than I had. Jennifer said they'd seen rats – 'We'd leave en masse if it wasn't for you,' she said. 'And we're getting some good laughs. But we won't come back next weekend – we're supposed to, if we're satisfactory.'

As I was finishing breakfast, Dick staggered up with a huge can of hot water, but advised me not to attempt a bath as he feared the hot water would melt Celina's decorations and they'd come off on me. He'd found me a bath towel almost as big as a bed sheet, very thin and a mass of holes. He said the ones in the Slepes' bathrooms were no better.

What could Cyprian have meant by saying, 'The great days will come again.'? The mind boggles at what it would cost to make Slepe habitable, let alone the cost of running it.

When I went down to Celina's studio she was already painting, wearing a white smock that reached to her feet and had no sleeves. She said, 'Good morning, don't talk until I've finished,' and went on painting at tremendous speed though with considerable care. There were already swirls of white and grey on the canvas, and she was now adding some pale pink. After a few minutes she stopped and said, 'It won't do. I *shall* have to put in a feature.'

I said, 'Do you mean that's me?'

'Yes, but it's not right. I must treat you realistically.'

I asked if I could see some of her realistic paintings and she said they were all in the picture gallery. She'd show me.

The gallery could never have been ideal for pictures as the whole of one side was taken up with tall windows through which the morning sun was flooding in quite dazzlingly. On the other long wall there were well over a dozen of Celina's canvases, all just swirls of colour. None of them was framed, but some were draped with different coloured chiffons. Celina led me to one draped in dark red and rapped out sharply, 'Who's that?'

The swirls were dark grey, white, and a dazzling blue. When I looked closely I saw that down in one corner, almost like a signature, was an admirably painted mouth. It was beautifully shaped, but there was something cruel about it. I said instantly, 'Cyprian.'

'There!' said Celina triumphantly, then looked troubled. 'Oh, dear, perhaps I'm getting *too* realistic.'

The paintings with their chiffon draperies were extraordinarily decorative – in fact, all the paintings were. I asked if she ever sold any and she said she'd had an exhibition years ago and sold everything in it, but the owners of the gallery had said they wouldn't show her work again unless she cut down her output. 'They found out I'd painted hundreds and hundreds. Though before we left England last year I had to paint on the walls because canvases cost quite a lot. But now the Count's given me enough of them to last until Cyprian is rich again. It was awful while we were abroad. Sometimes I painted on the walls of hotels and the proprietors didn't like it. One of them did, though; he let me paint all the attics and the stables.'

I then said, unwisely, 'Celina, I feel sure that if you were properly managed you could make a lot of money.'

She looked horrified. 'Oh, no, no, no! I didn't even like selling the paintings in my exhibition. Fancy you suggesting I should be commercial! Perhaps Cyprian's right about you.'

I asked what she meant and she said, 'Well, about it being so awful of you to be in that bath on television. But let's not talk about it. *I* think you're nice. Still, I won't finish painting you today. I shall know more about you by tomorrow. Then she waved a hand towards a group of chiffon-draped paintings and said, 'Tell me if you recognise anyone else.'

I saw that all these paintings had one tiny realistic feature, usually a mouth, but sometimes an eye and there was one ear. But I could only say that as I didn't know any of her friends—— She interrupted me. 'How about that one?'

It was a very pale canvas, white with some faint swirls of cream and yellow; indeed, they were barely formed enough to be called swirls. I said, 'There's nothing to get hold of. This isn't one of your realistic paintings.'

She told me to look closer. I let my eyes travel all over the canvas; although there was so little in it, I found it curiously pleasant. And at last I saw a shadowy mouth. It was barely visible and yet, once I'd noticed it, I was quite sure whose mouth it was.

I said, 'Roy?'

'Of course. Though the yellow's too strong.' Then she waved her long bare arms vaguely and said, 'Let's go out in the sunshine.'

As we walked along the gallery, she told me that every remaining ancestral painting had been sold before they left England. 'Not that they fetched much. The really valuable ones went before Cyprian inherited Slepe. The sad thing is that if we had them now they'd be worth millions, Cyprian says. Still, everything will be all right quite soon.'

When we were out of the picture gallery and on our way to the stairs she suddenly said, 'Oh, I've had an idea. Excuse me, please. I expect you can entertain yourself.' And then she actually ran, full tilt, towards her studio. I stared after her for a moment and then went downstairs to the hall. There was no one there, but I could hear Cyprian's voice in the library. No doubt another 'discussion' was taking place. The front door stood open. I decided to explore the garden.

But there *is* no garden and I didn't see any traces of one. There's just the park, dotted with old trees, some of them fallen. The grass has been allowed to grow right up to the house – you'd think someone would put some animals to graze on it. Soon the park will be a wilderness unless something's done.

I noticed there was a trodden pathway leading to the fake ruins so I followed it to them. There are small towers, and cloisters and an eighteenth-century colonnade – I soon realised that various periods had been jumbled together. At first I was fascinated, but one loses interest because one can't, as with real ruins, try to trace what has once been. Everything had been built just for effect. I was sitting on a stone seat, looking back at the Hall through a ruined arch when I saw someone coming along the trodden grassy path I'd come by. It was the Count.

I'd just as soon have dodged him. We'd barely exchanged one word and I hadn't particularly liked the look of him. But he'd seen me now and was smiling broadly. A few moments later he joined me on the stone seat.

We made some conversation about the ruins and I said how extraordinary it seemed to me that anyone should build them simply to make an interesting view from the Hall. The Count said that both the Hall and the ruins owed their existence to two madmen, the original owner and the architect he employed. 'They were, I believe close friends. All they were interested in was creating a string of palatial entertaining rooms, enough bedrooms for themselves and a few of their cronies, and a whole floor of servants' rooms.'

I said the servants now slept in the basement.

'In cellars,' said the Count. 'I've explored the whole house. Nothing in it makes sense. And it isn't a case of sacrificing convenience to beauty. Just look at the place! The proportions are atrocious. And yet our poor young host would lay down his life for it.'

I hadn't thought of Cyprian as young, but I suppose he seems so to the Count who is older than I'd realised at dinner. He hadn't said much then (well, who had except Cyprian?) but now he talked volubly, speaking of the love men can feel for their houses, and soon drifting into describing what had once been his own house in Poland – only it sounded more like a palace, indeed several palaces. He had lost everything during the war. Much had been destroyed and what remained was now shown to the public as a record of the bad old days. He admitted that, from some points of view, they had been bad but, to him, beauty could excuse almost everything – or didn't I agree?

I said I knew what he meant. All I really wanted to do was to encourage him to go on describing his Polish palace and his lost life there. This was partly because I found the details interesting, but also because I felt sympathy for him. He spoke with great gentleness, like a man remembering a much-loved, long-lost wife. Now I come to think of it, he never once mentioned a human being; it was only his house and the past that he spoke of. After a while he pulled himself up and said, 'You are a dangerously sympathetic lady. You make me talk too much about myself. Now we talk about you. Tell me, is your husband very ambitious?'

I was startled by the sudden change of subject and I found I'd no idea how to answer. I said at last, quite honestly, 'I don't really know. Naturally he wants to do well but . . . no, I wouldn't say he was drivingly ambitious.'

'Nor I,' said the Count, nodding and smiling. 'He would not, I think, be prepared to sacrifice everything for his career?'

I was wondering what to say, when the Count went on, 'Not that there should be any such need. He is already doing well in parliament, is he not?'

I said heartily, 'Yes, indeed. He's made a splendid start.'

'And he feels Cyprian Slepe will help him?'

'Well, it does help to know the right people. And Mr Slepe knows so many of them.'

'Ah,' said the Count, as if that explained everything. 'Well, I must return to him. I felt the need of a little recreation, which you have so kindly provided. I trust you forgive me for following you. We shall meet again at luncheon.'

He was up and off before I'd fully realised he was going. I sat there, going over our conversation. Had he really followed me? Just to have a casual conversation? And his very deliberate questions about Roy seemed to me odd.

I wandered round the ruins a little longer, then went back to the house. I went up to my room and then decided to explore some of the neighbouring rooms. All the ones I saw had been decorated by Celina but none of them were furnished. After a while a gong boomed and I went down to lunch.

Again we were treated to an almost non-stop monologue by Cyprian and, as at dinner, he ended by dismissing Celina and me. I resigned myself to another long session with her, but she excused herself on the ground of work. She didn't even arrange for any coffee. She said, 'I did so hope I was on the right lines at last, but I'm up against a brick wall. I just can't get him on canvas.' I asked who and she said, 'Roy, of course.' Then she left me flat.

I went into the hall hoping to find something to read, but there wasn't so much as a morning paper or a magazine. There was, however, a fairly comfortable chair so I sat down in it. I could dimly hear Cyprian holding forth in the library. He was still holding forth when I woke up well over an hour later. I thought 'I'm going to see if I can find a human being,' and went off to search for the kitchen.

I started from the dining-room, going through the door the 'servants' had come in by, and soon found a steep narrow staircase. I went down into a dimly lit stone-flagged passage, and at last found the kitchen. The door was open and Dick, Jennifer and Sylvia were sitting at one end of a long scrubbed table talking. As I went in, Sylvia looked up and said, 'That settles it. I'm going to tell her.'

They all got up and Dick offered me an old wicker armchair which creaked protestingly when I sat in it. Then the three of them grouped themselves round me and I gradually gathered they'd been having a long discussion as to what to do for the best. Sylvia said, 'I hate to admit I was eavesdropping and I know that repeating things so often makes mischief but still . . .'

Dick said, 'Well, you'll have to tell her now you've got as far as this.'

Sylvia then told me that, after she'd heard from Dick and Jennifer about Cyprian's monologues, she'd been upset to think she'd be leaving Slepe without so much as hearing his voice. 'You see, as housemaid I never get the chance to come into the dining-room. And then it struck me that they have all the windows in the library open and if I just stepped out onto the terrace, from the drawing-room . . . Anyway, I did it. And after a few minutes I heard something which set me back on my heels. Mr Slepe was talking to the Count – obviously Mr Mansfield wasn't there – and Mr Slepe said, "Of course my sister should never have invited her here. I've taken the greatest care to keep her out of things; indeed, I had every hope Roy would eventually break with her – he knows how unsuitable I consider her. But now that she's been here, heaven knows what ideas she may have got hold of. She'll definitely have to be eliminated."'

'Eliminated!' said Dick. 'The sheer impertinence of it!'

I said, 'It's all right, Dick. I already know Mr Slepe considers me unsuitable. It's largely due to that commercial I did, in the bath.'

'But that's lovely,' said Jennifer. 'I saw it only last week. They're running it again.'

'Unfortunately. Oh, not that I care, but I fear it will make things more difficult for my husband. Did Mr Slepe say how he proposed to eliminate me?'

'Not exactly,' said Sylvia, 'but I somehow gathered he meant to break things up between you and Mr Mansfield, especially now you're going back to the stage. He said he'd had that in mind when he suggested to Mr Mansfield that you should.'

I tried to think back. Surely Roy had approved of my acting again *before* the Slepes were back in England? But of course he'd been in touch with them. Had there been a deliberate plan? I made myself concentrate on what Sylvia was saying. 'Mr Slepe seemed worried in case you already knew more than you should about something he called "the scheme" and said you might tattle about it. He felt sure he'd given nothing away to you, but heaven knew what Celina might have said.'

I said angrily, 'Celina doesn't know what his bloody scheme is and neither do I.'

'The Count said he didn't think you did, but he quite agreed you should be kept out of things. And then he said he didn't think Cyprian was wise to have chosen your husband. He was a charming fellow but simply not the right material. "Why not let them both out?" said the Count. But Cyprian said No. He'd got to have at least one Member of Parliament and he could count on Roy doing as he was told. Everything would be all right once they got rid of you. Then your husband must have come into the room because Mr Slepe said, "Ah, Roy! Well, I trust you've solved all Celina's problems." I was too upset to listen any more so I dashed back here. Oh, goodness, perhaps I oughtn't to have told you.'

I said I was grateful to her and forewarned was forearmed, though if my husband allowed me to be got rid of he wouldn't be worth hanging on to. 'But I hardly think he'll agree.' I tried to say it as if I was taking the whole thing lightly.

'Of course he won't,' said Dick heartily. 'But it's as well you should know that Cyprian's trying to make mischief.'

'Let's have tea,' said Jennifer. 'We were told it wouldn't be needed upstairs. The Slepes don't take it so their guests don't get it.'

Then Mr Francis, 'the butler', came in and we'd barely been introduced before the cook arrived, a real genuine cook, like a large cottage loaf. She told me that nearly fifty years ago, when she was a kitchen-maid, she'd known a house like Slepe – 'But not as bad. That kitchen range! Really, I had to laugh. But we've managed, haven't we?' She beamed on the young people. 'They've turned it all into a joke.'

There was a loud jangle; one of a long row of iron bells had rung.

'Ah, the library,' said Mr Francis, rehearsing his lines ahead. 'You rang, sir?' He went off upstairs.

We were just settling down to tea when he came back.

'Great news, my children. This unforgettable weekend is ending a day early. Mr Slepe has to go back to London tomorrow morning. An urgent call. Though how it got through I can't imagine as the telephone isn't working.'

'Probably a lone rider came thundering cross country,' said Dick. He turned to me. 'Did you know about this?'

I said no, but I couldn't be more pleased – indeed, my spirits sprang up, but that was largely due to the company. That kitchen tea party's my one happy memory of Slepe. They were all such dears. One thing that impressed me was how well all the theatrical servants had behaved. Dick said the agency they worked for between theatrical jobs treated then with great consideration and they were determined not to let it down, even in such preposterous circumstances. As well as helping with dinner parties they did house-cleaning and Mr Francis sometimes did baby-sitting.

I told Dick and Jennifer and Sylvia I'd mention them to Rich, and Mr Francis too. He said there was no future for theatrical butlers and, though he occasionally got a few lines in television period plays, he was seriously thinking of taking lessons in real butling. The cook said she thought she could teach him enough to work with her as a team at London dinners. They were dead serious about it and I shouldn't be surprised if it came off.

When I left they were busy with preparations for dinner. There was a remarkably good smell coming from something in the oven. I looked back at that perfectly frightful kitchen and somehow – perhaps because of the open fire in that fantastic kitchen range – there was a macabre cosiness I was sorry to be leaving.

Sylvia was worried in case she had upset me and made mischief. Of course I reassured her. True, she had upset me, but the mischief was there quite independently of her. It had been there even before the Slepes returned to England. How long hadn't it been there?

Must stop recording. I heard a taxi draw up, looked out and saw Roy coming towards the house.

TAPE NINE

Wednesday, June 26th. 11.00 a.m.

Roy's just left the flat, won't be back until sometime the day after tomorrow. He told me he would be away with Cyprian Slepe and added, 'Please don't question me about it.' I'd no intention of doing so, after the talk we had when we returned to London on Sunday. More of that later.

Now back to Slepe on Saturday: after tea in the kitchen there seemed nothing to do but go up to my room and think indignant thoughts. Fairly soon Roy came in and told me about our visit being cut short. Of course I didn't tell him I already knew. I said I couldn't be more delighted. He said, 'I'm sorry, I'm sorry. Celina shouldn't have invited you here. This was intended to be just a working weekend for Cyprian, the Count and myself.'

I said, 'Working at what?', but he said he couldn't go into that and, anyway, he hadn't been working that afternoon as Celina had insisted on painting him. 'She burst into the library saying, "Cyprian, you must let me borrow him. You must or I shall go quite mad," ' – which I begin to think she is already. I spent nearly two hours in her studio, being stared at.'

'And painted?'

'Certainly not. She'd got a canvas on her easel covered with white paint and, every now and again, she'd dash at it and make some little mark, then paint it all out again, saying

"No, no, that's not it." At last she said it was hopeless and I'd better go back to Cyprian, which I thankfully did.'

I decided to cheer myself up by wearing the grandest dress Rich had lent me. When I went down to the hall Cyprian said 'That's a beautiful dress,' and I swear he said it with hatred, not admiration. Then he turned to Celina who was still wearing her floor-length, sleeveless white smock and said, 'How dare you come down to dinner looking like a stick of celery? Go and change at once.'

'I can't, I won't,' said Celina. 'I'm too miserable to think about silly things like clothes. I won't have any dinner.' She then bolted upstairs.

Cyprian turned to Mr Francis, who was hovering, and said, 'See that something is taken up to Miss Slepe's studio.'

'Certainly, sir,' said Mr Francis and then dug up one pearl from his memories of playing butlers. 'I will arrange for a cold collation.'

Dinner was worse than the night before – oh, not the food; again that nice cook had worked miracles – but the atmosphere. Cyprian actually ran out of conversation; I wondered if he was upset about Celina. If any of us spoke to him directly he seemed to be bringing his thoughts back from a long way off before he answered – very shortly.

After dinner I didn't wait for Cyprian to get rid of me. I said I was going to see how Celina was, and went. I found her lying flat on her back on the studio divan, with her long, naked arms outstretched as if she was being crucified. She turned her head to look at me and said, 'Take a look at Roy's portrait.'

There was a canvas on her easel, painted snow white all over. I said, 'But Celina, dear. There's nothing there.'

'Of course there is,' she said indignantly. 'There's all that white, exactly the shade of white I want.' She got up and gave the canvas a long look. 'Perhaps it *is* finished, really. I think I'll call it "Tabula Rasa".'

I asked what that meant exactly and she said she didn't know – exactly. 'That's why I like the sound of it. But I suppose it vaguely means something empty, erased. Well, God knows I've erased it often enough.'

I told her I had to go and pack. I suppose she *is* mad and yet I can't help feeling that in some strange way she's got a touch of genius. And I find I like her – whereas I loathe Cyprian.

Next morning Roy asked me what he ought to tip the butler. I don't know a thing about staying in country houses though I should have thought he would.

'Well, what did you give when you stayed here so often before?'

He said he'd been like one of the family then and had never tipped at all. I said he certainly must now, and I made sure Mr Francis, and the two footmen, got colossal tips. And I left plenty in my room – I felt certain the girls would share it with the cook. Roy looked a bit flabbergasted by the outlay.

The Count drove us to the station in his car. (The Slepes have not acquired a car since they got back to England. I gathered that if there was anything grander than a Rolls, they'd get it.) He and the Slepes were driving to London.

Roy and I scarcely spoke on the train. Both of us read the Sunday papers. Back at the flat I got together a scratch lunch. Roy went on reading newspapers and commented on them while we ate. It was only after I'd cleared the table and brought in coffee that he said, 'There's something I need to get clear and I'm anxious not to hurt you. From now on I shall have to spend a lot of time with the Slepes – that is, with Cyprian – and I shall have to be on my own. I take it you'll hardly mind not being included?' He managed a hint of a smile.

I said, 'Nothing would persuade me to be included. Honestly – and I say this quite sincerely and with no bitterness – would you like to go and live with them, as you once did?'

He must have been silent for a good half minute before he said, 'Of course not. They do plan to have a room for me at their flat, but I shall only use it if there's some important discussion that goes on very late.'

I suddenly lost patience, though I made myself speak quietly. 'Roy, how can they possibly afford an expensive flat? Surely you took in the state of affairs at Slepe? They haven't any money.'

To my surprise, he didn't contradict me. He merely said, 'I know they haven't now, but they will have very soon. When they left England Cyprian felt he'd just have to let Slepe go. You remember what he said at dinner on Friday, about leaving it to decay? That's what he expected to happen. But now all that's changed. He'll be able to restore it to glory.'

I said I didn't believe it had ever been glorious; it's really just a monstrous Folly. 'Still I can understand Cyprian's feelings for his ancestral home. But restoring it would cost a fabulous amount, not to mention the cost of refurnishing. It looks as if everything of real value has been sold. And how about running it, in this day and age?'

'Cyprian's not of this day and age. He has a timeless genius. Surely you've realised that after hearing him talk?'

Never before have I seen Roy look fanatical. I forced myself to be tactful and said I did realise Cyprian was brilliant. But how was he suddenly going to make a colossal fortune?

'He is if he says he is. Anyway, the money's only important because it will leave him free for his work. It's all a question of idealism, of vision – one has to trust. I didn't always, not on our brief meetings abroad. He wasn't able to tell me everything then.'

'And he has now? You really believe in this scheme of his that's going to save the world?'

Roy looked staggered. 'I've told you nothing about that.

I've never said one word.'

I said hastily, 'No, of course you haven't. It was just something Celina mentioned and then said she shouldn't have and, anyway, she'd no idea what the scheme was.'

'Of course she hasn't. We mustn't go on talking. All I can tell you is that I want to feel free to follow Cyprian's star. You see, quite apart from any question of idealism, I want to get on. What I achieved was due to Cyprian and after he left England I achieved nothing more.'

I saw in a flash that this was true. And I also saw that he'd exchanged Cyprian for me and I'd done nothing to help him. I couldn't stimulate him into making an impression politically. I couldn't introduce him to important people. And what right had I to judge Cyprian? Half the time I didn't understand what he was talking about. Compared with him I was a moron—and a moron who appeared in a bath on television. No wonder he saw me as a menace to Roy's career.

I said, 'All right. You must do whatever you think right. What's my best way to help you?'

He drew a sigh of relief, 'Oh, my dear, I'm so grateful. All I ask is that you should leave me free and ask no questions. None of this makes any difference between us really.'

Like hell it does, I thought but I simply asked if he wanted to go on living at the flat. He said yes, but he might be away a lot and couldn't always let me know if he'd be in for meals. I said now I was working I couldn't be on hand to cook for him if he turned up unexpectedly, but I'd make sure cold food was always available. He said he was glad I was back in the theatre and he'd never again stand in my way. He then added something which nearly wrecked my determination to be patient. 'And please do appear on television if you want to. Cyprian doesn't think it will matter now.'

I said, 'Thanks. Anyway, I'll try to keep out of baths. Which reminds me, I'd like one now. It wasn't any too easy to keep clean at Slepe.'

Then the telephone rang and he answered it and then said he had to go out. He didn't say where and I didn't ask. From now on, I'd ask him no questions. Anyway, I was near enough to the telephone to recognise Cyprian's elegant, high-pitched voice.

After I'd done the washing-up, I ran a bath and spent a good long time in it, feeling reasonably cheerful. I'd now decided on a course of action. I must lift my thoughts off Roy and get on with my own life. Once I'd settled down at the theatre I'd set about getting television work; I could combine it with understudying – though if Rich really had a part for me in one of his autumn productions perhaps I'd stick to the theatre. The great thing was that life now held some promise.

But after I got out of the bath I felt less cheerful. Was I simply playing into Cyprian's hands by making no claims on Roy, simply allowing myself to be 'eliminated'? I decided to talk to myself on the tape-recorder. As well as getting my thoughts clear, I wanted to describe Slepe while it was fresh in my mind.

I unlocked the basket and began moving the tapes Lyn and I made years ago. I'd stuck to Tim's advice and kept them on top of the basket, with all my new tapes underneath. When I picked up the tape of Shakespeare's Sonnets, I remembered an argument Lyn and I once had about 'Let me not to the marriage of true minds admit impediment.' Lyn said you couldn't judge if you were involved in a marriage of true minds, as long as you were confused by physical love. Once she stopped being physically in love, she stopped being in love at all – so how could she ever come by a marriage of true minds? I felt sure I'd know at once if what I felt was real love and I never thought I felt it for Rich. But I did feel it for Roy, almost from our first meeting. Well, if so, was I cheerfully preparing to go my own way and let him go his? No doubt it was a way of avoiding suffering, but that was a cheap thing to do if you really cared for anyone. And I certainly couldn't lay claim to the love that 'looks on tempests, and is never shaken'.

Well, I ought at least to have a shot at it, which meant I must still hang onto the suffering – and there it suddenly was again, as alive as ever. I put the tape-recorder back in the basket; if I used it, I should just moan on and on, not describe Slepe. What I needed now was not so much to give Roy another chance, as to give my feelings for him another chance.

During the evening I tried and failed to telephone Tim. I haven't been in touch with him since he drove me to rehearsal last week. Not once have I seen his taxi in the square. I watched television, went to bed early and put the light out before Roy came back. I fell asleep full of good intentions towards him – all of which dwindled next day when he told me he was going to spend the afternoon flat-hunting with the Slepes. They'd heard of a penthouse in Park Lane.

Anyway, once he'd left the house I could settle down at this tape-recorder and begin describing Slepe. Then I went down to the theatre for my first official night as an understudy. There were three lots of flowers at the stage door: from Rich, from Lyn, and – believe it or not – from the Count! I hadn't realised he even knew I was starting a job. There was no address on his card so I haven't yet been able to thank him; not that I mind much, seeing that Sylvia overheard him advise Cyprian to get rid of both Roy and me. He must be an old hypocrite.

I enjoyed the evening, chatting with my room-mate who is a dear. When Rich arrived with champagne, she drank a glass and then tactfully excused herself. Before he left, Rich said, 'Supper, no?' I shook my head and he said, 'I wasn't exactly counting on it.' Dear Rich, I do like him so much. In some ways I'm nearer having a marriage of true minds with him than I've ever had with Roy.

Rich's visit wouldn't be the cause of scandal and concern as he's always dropping into people's dressing-rooms (if not always bearing champagne). It's one of the reasons he's so popular with his companies. After he'd gone it struck me there really isn't any reason why I shouldn't have supper with him and I felt it all the more when I got back to the flat and Roy wasn't there. Still, I can't stop feeling that if he gets in tired and hungry, I ought to be there to feed him. Yesterday, Tuesday, he spent some time in the flat and was quite pleasant but also quite uncommunicative, and again he wasn't in when I got back from the theatre. For once, I didn't hear him come in – a good sign; I wasn't lying awake thinking about him. This morning, as I think I've already recorded, he's gone off until Friday with Cyprian Slepe. He just sprang it on me – he'd packed his own suitcase.

Well, that brings me to this morning, Wednesday, and there's really nothing else I want to record – which leaves me at rather a loose end. I've come to think of recording as a duty; also I do find it helps to clear my mind, as Tim said it would. Tim! It's now on my conscience that I haven't been able to get in touch with him. . . . I've just looked out of the window and his taxi's actually there. I'm going down to ask him to drive me somewhere – or would he, as Roy's safely away, come up here to talk?

5.00 p.m.
Tim really was very odd this morning. He wouldn't come up to the flat, told me to jump into the taxi quickly and not to talk until he told me I could. Then he drove towards the West End, but soon turned into a back street and then turned again and again before he pulled up in a mews, got into the back with me and told me to go ahead. I asked him if he'd feared we were being followed. He said, 'Could have been, but we weren't. Now tell me about the weekend.'

I plunged in, describing Slepe, but he cut me short, saying

he already knew it was in a bad state of repair, (odd, that, as *I* didn't know until I saw it) and would I tell him about the other guests. I said there was only the Count and as soon as I mentioned him Tim got interested and wanted a full description. When I asked him why he was interested, he said the Count sounded like someone he'd heard of, but there were probably plenty of foreign counts around. Actually, there was one in the book by Tim I read, so I wondered if it was the thriller-writer in him taking over.

He wasn't interested in Celina's paintings or in the stage people acting as servants; in fact, I felt my story was falling flat – until I got to meeting the Count in the ruins. Then I was asked to relay the whole conversation. One can't, really, but I did my best. Tim wanted to know if I'd described it more fully when I was tape-recording – I'd told him I'd had quite a session at that. He also wanted to know if I'd heard anything which threw any light on Roy's suspicious behaviour. I said I'd come to the conclusion that, apart from the passing of the two packages, Roy's behaviour wasn't suspicious. He was simply involved in some political plan of Cyprian's which was still a secret. Cyprian was determined to keep me out of it and I couldn't care less. I'd now undertaken not to ask Roy questions. I'm beginning to feel I ought not to have talked about him so much to Tim, these last weeks. Weeks! It feels like months. It's really only two weeks today since I followed Roy to Regent's Park.

Quite abruptly Tim said he would have to take me home as he had an appointment to call for someone. I suggested he might drive me down to the theatre tonight, but he said he wouldn't be free. But I could telephone him late tonight. I can do that, as Roy won't be home.

I found Tim puzzling today; some of the time he seemed preoccupied. Perhaps I'm beginning to bore him. But he gave me a particularly nice smile when we parted and he said, '*Do* telephone.'

I've just remembered I didn't tell him what Sylvia overheard, but that wouldn't have particularly interested him, and I really covered it by saying that Cyprian wanted to keep me out of his plans for Roy.

I've taken to having a sort of high-tea meal before going to the theatre. I'll go and get it.

TAPE TEN

Thursday, June 27th. 10.00 a.m.

I'm not sure I can bring myself to talk. Lyn says I must, both to get things clear in my own mind and to get them clear for her. I told her everything last night but she says I was barely coherent, and I must, I must remember fully while I still can. But to talk about last night means plunging back into the horror. God knows I don't want to, but I'll try.

Calmly, now. Go back to when you arrived at the theatre. There was a large bouquet of red roses waiting for me at the stage-door. The florist's envelope with my name on was inside the cellophane wrapping so I didn't open it until I was up in my dressing-room. As I undid the cellophane I wondered if the roses could conceivably be from Roy; I hardly thought Rich would send me more flowers so soon.

The card inside the envelope said, 'Would you please do me the great honour of having supper with me tonight? Apart from the pleasure it will give me, it is of the utmost importance to you that I should have a chance to talk to you. I will call at the stage-door at ten-thirty to receive your answer – and, I hope, await your company.' It was signed by the Count.

My first thought was that at ten-thirty I'd go down to the stage-door and explain that I couldn't come because I had a prior engagement. Then it struck me he would ask me to come on some other night. And I didn't want to, ever. I didn't believe he had anything important to tell me and, as it was only two days since he had sent me the first bouquet, I frankly thought he was merely paying court to me in an old-fashioned stage-door-johnnie way. Perhaps he thought that, as I was not to have any share in 'the scheme', he could console me. He was old enough to remember the days when an 'actress' – the word lived in perpetual inverted commas – could be wooed with roses and, later, some jewel in a velvet-lined case.

I decided to write a note for the stage-doorkeeper to hand to him. My room-mate had a pad of paper and envelopes. I described the Count to her and she laughed and said, 'My dear, what you're missing! He might set you up in a discreet villa in St John's Wood.' I made the note courteous, thanked him for his lovely flowers and his interest, and said I hoped he would understand that I couldn't accept his kind invitation, because I always felt I had to hurry home to be with my husband on his return from the House. I hoped the mention of my husband would indicate that I was a virtuous wife, not to be tempted by foreign noblemen. Barbara and I had a merry time imagining Edwardian seductions in private rooms with gilt furniture and red velvet sofas – not that the Count's old enough for that, really; I should think he's only in his middle sixties. And then I took the note down to the stage-doorkeeper.

A bit before 10.30 we put the dressing-room lights out and opened the window. Our room's high up and quite a way from the stage-door, but you can see it if you lean out. Barbara was so dead set on seeing the Count that she'd passed up catching her early train. She'd decided he'd arrive in an opera hat and a scarlet-lined cloak. She looked down and reported he was already waiting. Then she saw the stage-doorkeeper come out and hand the note. The Count read it and I hoped he'd go off quietly, but he went in through the stage-door. We closed our window and put our lights on again. A few minutes later, up comes the stage-doorkeeper.

'The foreign gentleman's very much upset. He says will you please come down and see him?'

I wasn't going to have an argument at the stage-door, so I told the stage-doorkeeper to say I'd gone, but he said he'd already admitted that I was still there.

'Well, tell him you can't find me now and I must have gone out of the front of the house.'

I was determined not to leave until I knew the coast was clear so, as soon as the stage-doorkeeper had gone down, we put the lights off again and Barbara looked out of the window. She soon saw the Count walking away. Then she said, 'No, he's turned round. He's coming back to the stage-door. Perhaps he's going to force his way in.'

'Well, he'll be out of luck if he does, because I *will* go out of the front of the house.'

'That's right,' said Barbara, laughing. 'You leave me to face him.'

The curtain had been down some little while and already the stage was deserted. I was afraid the pass door might be locked but it wasn't. There wasn't a sign of life in the auditorium and already the dustsheets were spread over the seats. There's a pretty quick exodus of staff at curtain fall. Some of the house lights were still on, but they went off before I reached the foyer. However, there was a glimmer of light at the end of the passage leading to the stalls and I managed quite well. But when I reached the foyer the lights were off – the glimmer I'd seen was from the street lights, shining through the glass doors. I dashed to them. Surely they wouldn't be locked as early as this? But they were.

My first thought was that I'd go up to the office. But the stairs to it are outside the foyer, and I wasn't going to trust myself to that lift, especially in the dark. And I remembered then that the office staff only stays on late when Rich is there and I knew he'd gone to a provincial try-out. Obviously I must go back to the pass door. I tried to visualise my way. The long passage to the stalls slopes and there were two short flights of steps – or was it three, and how soon did they come? I should have to grope my way with the utmost care. Then I remembered I had a torch in my bag, the tiny one Tim gave me the night he saw me up the stairs to the flat. I'd never used it. Well, God bless Tim, I thought as I snapped it on.

I still had to go carefully as the sloping part of the passage is deceptive. And just as I came to the first steps, I had the shock of my life. From the stalls there came a hoarse whisper of, 'Mrs Mansfield.'

I snapped the torch off and stood stock still. I was instantly sure who was there. It was the Count.

How had he managed it? Presumably he had slipped in from the street just before the foyer doors were closed and got down to the stalls on the far side as I was leaving them. He couldn't know I was there – or could he? He just might have seen me as I left the stalls.

I had a moment of panic. He must be mad to follow me like that. I could think of no way out of the theatre except by going back through the pass door – which meant showing myself in the stalls – but I could, at least, get further away from him. I got back to the foyer fairly easily by the glimmer of the street lights and, once there, I made for the stairs to the dress circle. I felt I could safely use my torch at first, but I snapped it off near the top of the stairs, groped my way into the back of the circle, then stood still and listened.

After a few seconds, I heard the Count again: 'Mrs Mansfield, please listen. I *know* you're there.'

So he *had* seen me! He was now shining a torch upwards from the stalls and, though I felt sure I must be out of his line of sight, I crouched down behind the barrier at the back of the circle. I tried to think and it was then a frightful idea struck me. I remembered Tim, the night we first met, saying that if Roy was involved in espionage his masters could be ruthless, and I'd said, 'Do you mean they might bump me off, like on television?' Was that what Cyprian meant by saying I must be eliminated? I'd ruled out anything to do with espionage because I was sure that Cyprian would never work for Russia, but other countries employed spies, surely. Of course I couldn't reason clearly, my whole mind was whirling with just flashes of ideas and I felt sick with fear. How, how could I get out of the theatre?

The Count was still searching for me with his torch and whispering, louder now, almost calling, though I only took in that he was begging me to answer him. Then there was silence and no more flashes of light. I guessed he had gone out of the stalls. Did he intend to search the theatre? If he got as far as the dress circle he would spot me instantly. Could I hide somewhere? Could I get to the Ladies and lock the door or, if there was no lock, bolt myself into a lavatory? I had a dim memory of where the Ladies was, but could I reach it without using my torch? If he started to come up the stairs he'd soon see any glimmer of light. I must grope my way, hoping to find a door handle.

And then I noticed two squares paler than the darkness, and remembered there was a bar over the foyer at the back of the dress circle. The upper parts of the doors were of glass and there was a faint glimmer from street lighting. I dashed towards them and through them.

The bar is quite large. I remember rehearsing there once in my early days at the theatre. There was just enough light to show me a door open onto some stairs which I guessed led to the upper circle. I risked using my torch and dashed up them.

My idea was that there would be a fire-escape for the upper circle. I could only find it by using my torch, but if the Count really was searching the whole theatre I must be well ahead of him and I'd just have to risk it.

The upper circle is very large; at one time the top part was the gallery. The door I came in by was low down and as I shone my torch I saw a steeply rising tier of seats, with an arrow pointing to fire-escape right at the top. When I was half way up, I heard the Count on the staircase I'd just come up by. He was calling – loudly, now: 'Mrs Mansfield, wait! You *must* listen to me!' I got to the top just as the beam from his torch shone up on me.

The doors to the fire-escape were the kind that are marked 'Push Bar to Open' and I had to struggle with them. The Count was well on his way up behind me when I got them open and stepped out – for all I saw I might have been stepping into space but I was, actually, on a roof top. There was just enough light from the street below to show me the parapet, but all around me was blackness. The tiny beam of my torch travelled no distance and I'd no way of telling where the fire-escape stairs were. No doubt during a performance there would be lights and directions. For me there was only windy darkness.

Then my torch beam showed me a place where the line of the parapet was broken by a solid mass in which was a dimly-lit window. Just then I heard the Count wrestling with the fire-escape doors – I'd managed to slam them together behind me. I dashed towards the lighted window, tripped over something and dropped the torch. Its light went out and I didn't dare stop to grope for it. I went on, full tilt, towards the window. When I got to it there was enough light for me to see it was open onto a landing, but I'd have gone through it even into someone's bedroom. I'd just clambered in when I heard the Count get the doors open, and I was round the first bend of some stairs when I heard him shout, 'Mrs Mansfield! For God's sake don't go.' After that I could still hear him shouting, but not what he was saying because I was racing down the stairs.

Except for the dimly-lit staircase the building seemed to be in darkness. For a moment I feared I was in an office block and the street door would be locked. Then I heard music and voices and saw a line of light under a ground floor door. I was in a small block of flats and the street door was open.

But even when I was out in the street I didn't feel safe. It was a quiet backstreet, with no traffic; there didn't seem any hope of getting a taxi quickly. The Count, with his strong torch, would soon find the fire-escape stairs, think I had gone down them and come after me. Where would they come out? My exit through the block of flats had thrown my sense of direction out of gear and I couldn't even place where the theatre was. The uppermost thought in my mind was, 'Get away! Get away anywhere!' I ran.

Soon, thank God, I came to a street where there were some brightly-lit restaurants and a nightclub, outside which a taxi was delivering some people. I ran even faster, calling, 'Wait for me, please wait!' The driver heard and waited. As I got in, he said, 'Someone chasing you?' I said, 'You could say that.'

'Some nasty types round here,' said the driver and, after that, was mercifully silent.

Oh, the relief of being in that taxi! But it was only momentary for I was sure now that I was in danger. For one sick moment I imagined what it would have been like if the Count had cornered me on the roof. What a perfect place to 'eliminate' me! He could have forced me over the parapet, then made his get away down the fire-escape. I loathe heights; even imagined heights make me feel dizzy. I thought of myself wrestling with him, the fall, the crash——! Then I pulled myself together. If the Count had been ordered to kill me, he would try again. How could I protect myself? As soon as I was in the flat I would ring Tim. He had again and again warned me of possible danger, but so vaguely. Tonight I had been in real danger, within inches of death.

When I paid the taxi-driver he said, 'Well, here you are, home safe and sound. If you ask me, ladies oughtn't to be alone at night in London, not these days. And you being a celebrity makes it worse.'

I stared at him. 'What?'

'Recognised you in a flash. Saw you only last night, in the bath.'

That damned TV bath!

I opened the front door of the house and pressed the light switch. As I closed the door I thought of Tim's little torch that I'd dropped on the roof. I'd never bothered to use it if the lights went off before I reached the flat – I knew the last stairs so well. But it had certainly saved my life that night. How extraordinary to realise that for once I meant the phrase literally.

I must have gone up the stairs fairly slowly as the lights went off just as I reached the third floor. I stood still for a second and that very instant I heard a sound in the old bathroom – a footstep, then another – I was sure that was what they were – inside the bathroom. For a split second I thought of going downstairs again, but I couldn't go quickly in pitch darkness. My best chance was to go up to the flat. I would bolt the door and then telephone the police.

How had the Count got there ahead of me? For of course it must be the Count. I was back in the nightmare.

I always get my key out of my bag while the lights are on, so I had it ready in my hand. I got up the last flight of stairs without stumbling, fumbled for the keyhole for what seemed like a life time, then I was in. I snapped the lights on and shot the two bolts. Now for the police.

Then I hesitated. Was I really sure I'd heard someone in the old bathroom? It seemed incredible that the Count could have got ahead of me and got through the locked front door of the house. And if he was in the bathroom he must have heard me coming upstairs. Why hadn't he come out and caught me before I reached the comparative safety of the flat?

I listened. No sound came from below. The last thing I

wanted to do was to get the police on a wild goose chase. And if I sent for them, I should have to go down and let them in, which meant passing that bathroom. If the Count *was* there, he could drag me in and kill me, then get away by the fire-escape which could be reached from the bathroom window. I listened again. Still no sound from below.

I would telephone Tim. I might be imagining there was someone in the bathroom, but there was no imagination about what had happened at the theatre. Tim would tell me what to do to protect myself. Should I ring Scotland Yard? Tim would know the right department. Even as I thought about this I realised I should involve the Slepes and, through them, Roy. But perhaps I could actually *save* Roy. Surely he could have no idea what kind of people Cyprian and the Count must be? Anyway, I'd talk to Tim.

I dialled his number but could get no reply. I looked at my watch. It felt like the middle of the night to me, but it was only twenty past eleven. Tim had said he would be in late. I'd wait a bit before dialling again.

I went into the hall and listened again. Still no sound from below. And there were good strong bolts on the front door. I'd make some coffee. The kitchen door was open. I put out my hand towards the light switch – and that instant saw at the window the figure of a man, outlined against the sky. Oh, God, what a fool I'd been! The Count had discovered he could come up via the fire-escape.

He stooped, to lift up the sashed window. I stepped back, out of his sight, but I should have to step into it again to reach the front door and he would be in the flat before I could get the bolts drawn back, let alone get downstairs. I had just one chance. There is a little curtained alcove in the hall, where we hang coats. I slipped into it as I heard the window raised. I felt sure he would go straight towards the lighted sitting-room. He did, and I instantly came out of the alcove, snatched my bag from the hall table and dashed into the kitchen. With any luck I should get down the fire-escape while he searched the flat.

I was in deadly terror of falling down the iron stairs, but there was more light than I expected, from the mews below. I was down to the first floor before I heard sounds from above. I still had the last section to push down. If it had stuck I should have had to jump. But it worked all right. I could hear heavy footsteps pounding down from above as I reached the mews. Surely I could run faster than the old Count?

I was some way along the mews when I heard a loud bump and then a scream. I guessed what had happened. The bottom section had swung up – it's supposed to – and the Count must have failed to push it down; he'd either fallen or jumped. I went on running. The next second there was a shout of, 'Help, help! Oh, God, I've broken my leg. Come back, please! I've a message from your husband.'

That wasn't the Count's voice. It was a high, shrill voice with no foreign accent. I stopped and turned. I could just see a man lying on the ground. He was trying to get up but sank back, groaning. I thought, 'Well, if he can't walk, he can't do much to me,' and started to go back. A moment later, there was a flash, a bang and something whistled past my ear. I thought, 'My God, I'm being fired at,' and turned and ran for my life. There was another bang and another whistling sound but this time I was further away. A moment later I turned the corner of the mews.

There had been a second – I suppose it must have been when he half raised himself to fire at me – when a street light in the mews had shone on the man's head. He had shoulder-length fair hair. It was the creature Roy had met in Regent's Park.

I went on running. I thought the man was hurt, but he might have been shamming or might recover enough to come after me, and I was in a deserted street, no taxi in sight. Where was the nearest police station? I'd no idea, also I dreaded talking to the police, all the more as the man had said he had a message from Roy. Should I make for the Underground? But suppose the man followed me into it, so easy to push anyone onto the line. And anyway, where should I go?

And then I suddenly knew. Along the street, surprisingly late, came a bus. I'd have jumped on any bus, but this bus was the bus of buses for me for I knew it went past Lyn's flat. I would go to Lyn and I would now tell her everything.

TAPE ELEVEN

Thursday, June 27th (continued). 11.30 a.m.

Lyn was right. Recording all this on her tape-recorder has made things clearer to me – and much clearer to her, she says, now I've just played the tape back to her. Last night, as well as being incoherent, I had to try to give her the story from the beginning. I must have been wildly confusing. Now she wants to listen to all the earlier tapes and I'll listen with her. This means going back to the flat for them, which I dread, but Lyn will come with me; anyway I'll have to collect some clothes. It's a blessing Roy's away until tomorrow so he won't know I've left. I was angry because he didn't tell me where he was going; now I'm thankful, because I can't get in touch with him. What could I say, feeling as I do now?

Lyn was marvellous last night. I literally fell on her when she opened the front door and as I'm bigger than she is I nearly knocked her down. Oh, the relief of talking to her at last.

We went on till nearly four in the morning. Lyn kept making fresh coffee. She can't possibly have a clear picture but she says it's enough to go on with, 'More than enough,' she added grimly.

She's now gone out to buy food for our lunch. Mercifully she has no rehearsal this morning as there's a matinée. She told me not to open the door to *anyone*. She also told me to go on tape-recording. She thinks it has a 'therapeutic' effect on me (and I did feel steadier after talking) also that, without realising it, I may remember something valuable. That was Tim's idea, too. Tim! About two a.m. I remembered I'd never rung him. I didn't feel I could disturb him then or face telling him the whole story. I rang this morning but got no reply – it was really too late by the time I thought of it. Anyway, it doesn't matter. I keep thinking he'll worry about me but he won't; there was nothing specially for him to worry about when I talked to him yesterday.

I didn't wake up until nine o'clock this morning. Lyn had made me take a sleeping pill; she said if I didn't my brain would go on working and I shouldn't be fit to cope with life today. I've always disliked the idea of sleeping pills, but I must say I woke up feeling well – and most surprisingly cheerful. That was largely due to finding myself here with Lyn instead of at the flat.

Lyn brought me breakfast and then, as soon as I was dressed, settled me down with her tape-recorder. At first, the fact that it wasn't *my* machine made me absurdly self-conscious. But I soon talked myself into forgetting that and just relived last night. There's nothing more I want to say about that. In fact, there's not much more I want to say about anything until Lyn and I have listened to all the tapes together . . . Oh, there *is* something I want to say: I told Lyn last night that I didn't believe Roy knew I was going to be attacked and I still don't believe it. He may have been fooled, pretty well hypnotised by Cyprian Slepe, but not to the extent of agreeing that I should be killed.

One thing I know: I can't go on living at the flat. Can I tell Roy, when he returns – simply speak to him on the telephone – that I'm staying with Lyn, and not say one word about what happened last night? If I tell him, I shall be accusing his associates, expecting him to do something about it. And suppose he did know they planned to eliminate me? I find I'm frightened. Will the Count and the man who fired at me try again?

When I go to the flat today I can leave a note for Roy to find when he comes home tomorrow. Then I needn't even speak to him on the telephone. . . . I've just realised that I do doubt him. I'm not going to record any more. I'm just working up doubts and fears.

Later. 5.30 p.m.
Lyn got back by twelve and said we'd have lunch at once – bacon and eggs, toast, marmalade and coffee. In the old days we often had that meal, breakfast for lunch. She kept talking about the old days; I'm sure she did it to get my mind off the present and, though she didn't manage that, I did get just a whiff of feeling that the present was like one of the adventures we used to have when we started to make our way in London – not that anyone then tried to kill us.

Thinking of that made me tell Lyn I might be involving her in danger by staying with her. I must go to a hotel. She wouldn't hear of it, but said what I needed – what we both needed now – was police protection.

I told her I couldn't get that without going to the police, which would involve Roy. 'Besides, Tim said if I told anyone it would involve me in danger.' I didn't say he'd particularly told me not to tell *her*.

She said, 'Listen, darling. If there was one part of your story that didn't make sense last night it was this Tim business. I'm sure he's a good, kind lad and a splendid taxi-driver *and* a thriller writer, but he's been giving you rotten advice.'

'He hasn't. Can't you see that if Roy's involved with espionage I'd be in danger if anyone found out that I knew?'

'You can't be in any worse danger than you are now – with two people trying to assassinate you in one night.'

'Tim wasn't to know that would happen. Anyway, I won't have you sneering at him.'

'I haven't sneered one sneer. I'm very grateful to him for

trying to help you. But you must admit he's not qualified to advise you now.'

'Well, who the hell is?'

'That,' said Lyn, 'has been arranged.'

'Lyn, you couldn't, you haven't——'

But I felt quite sure she had. Among the men with whom she is, or has been, 'just good friends' (though I think, in this case, the word 'friends' is technically correct) is someone fairly high up at Scotland Yard.

She went on smugly, 'I rang Mike when I went out to buy our lunch – from a call box, so that I wouldn't disturb your recording.'

'And so I wouldn't stop you.' But actually, I was relieved.

'He'll be here by the time we get the lunch cleared away. My dear, he's avid – like a cat offered cream. You see, he happens to be in Special Branch.'

He arrived as we were finishing the washing up. Lyn, introducing, said, 'Nan, this is Mike. A very reliable type.'

He looked it, but more than anything he looked ordinary. I don't know many ordinary-looking men. Roy, Cyprian Slepe, Rich; the men at the theatre – hardly any actors look ordinary. And Tim, with his young hair and slightly-ageing face, certainly doesn't. Mike has a solid look, neither plain nor good-looking, rather short hair, a conventional suit neither cheap nor particularly well-cut. Yes, indeed, a reliable type.

Lyn must have told him quite a lot on the telephone. He didn't ask me to go back to the beginning of my suspicions. He just questioned me about last night, taking me step by step, in a way that only called for brief answers. He made no comments, just went on asking questions. Everything I said sounded melodramatic and when I got to the end, where I jumped on the bus and came to Lyn, I thought: 'This is it, the scene I always hate in books or on TV. He doesn't believe me.' I turned on him and said, 'Damn you, it's true.'

He looked startled. Then he smiled, put his hand in his pocket and took out my pocket torch. 'We found it on the roof, and two spent bullets in your mews. Oh, I believe you all right.'

'Was that horrible man still lying in the mews this morning?'

'No, he wasn't. And we haven't yet traced that any man with long, dyed fair hair has been treated at a hospital. Now about your husband. Are you holding anything back? If you are, remember you may pay with your life for it. Don't you really know where he is?'

'I only know he said he'd be with Cyprian Slepe. Did Lyn hand that on to you?'

'She did. Our Lyn's a fast talker and thank God she speaks clearly on the telephone. Well, I've already made inquiries. Slepe Hall's closed up. Did your husband have his passport with him?'

'I've no idea. He didn't let me pack for him, as I usually do.'

Mike said, 'We must go to your flat and look for it. And please, Mrs Mansfield – Nan, if I may, I do beg you to think of me as a friend as well as a policeman – please let me bring back those tapes and listen to them.'

'Can you force me to, by law?'

He smiled. 'I don't really know. It's a nice point. But don't let's put it to the test. Think of it this way: if your husband's innocent, nothing you've said will incriminate him. What's more, he may be in danger himself.'

It was the first time I'd thought of that. I said I supposed he might be. 'He might not know what he was involved in. I'm sure he wouldn't knowingly have anything to do with espionage. And much as I loathe Cyprian Slepe I can't believe he would – not on behalf of Russia.'

Mike said, 'Last night's attempts on you seem to me too inefficient for Russia.'

Lyn, who had kept quiet a long time, erupted into the

conversation. 'It's drug pushing on a huge scale. Cyprian would have no conscience about that.'

'Bright girl,' said Mike, with the kind of heartiness I thought would annoy her. But she barely frowned. She was smug with satisfaction at having produced him just when he was needed.

He said, 'Now we're going to your flat, Nan. And you're going to let me have those tapes, aren't you?'

'I suppose so. Though I bet they'll be a waste of your time. I can't have put in clues I don't even know about. And they're horribly personal.'

'Policemen,' said Mike, 'are like doctors and priests – only much more impersonal.'

While we were driving to the flat I felt sick at the thought of going into it. I wasn't frightened, with Lyn and Mike with me. It was just the memory of last night. I hoped Tim would be in the square so that I could have a word with him, but there was no sign of him or his taxi.

The house seemed perfectly normal, with the front door open and voices and typewriter tappings coming from the various offices. Up in the flat the only signs of an intruder were that every cupboard was flung open and the curtain in the hall alcove torn down. There are so few hiding places that I was lucky to have started down the fire-escape before the man came after me.

I hunted for Roy's passport but couldn't find it. That might mean that he's abroad now but, as I told Mike, there's nothing unusual about that as he often goes to the Continent. Then we went into my little room and I unlocked the basket. I reached down to move the old recordings, which I always keep on top of my new ones, and then I stopped dead. I was instantly sure the tapes had been disturbed. Last Sunday, when I put Shakespeare's Sonnets back I put them to one side, as a reminder to listen to them when I was in a better mood. I left them where they were when I recorded on

Monday and Tuesday and yesterday. When I opened the basket this afternoon they were back among the other old recordings.

I told Mike. He asked me to think back – was I absolutely sure? I was – and am. Just before I closed the basket yesterday afternoon I particularly noticed the sonnets all on their own.

Mike questioned me. How many people had known about the tapes? Only Tim. Couldn't Roy have known? I remembered that one day – last Monday, I think – he came into the flat while I was still recording and I told him I was rehearsing my part. Suppose he didn't believe me? But it was only yesterday that I saw the sonnets just where I had left them – and he's been away. He might have come back while I was at the theatre yesterday evening, but he couldn't have had my key to the padlock on the basket and if he'd broken into it, wouldn't there have been signs of that?

'You must have made a mistake,' said Lyn. 'It isn't as if you deliberately baited a trap.'

We were still discussing it when I happened to look out of the window and saw that Tim's taxi had arrived in the square. I said I must go down and speak to him. Mike said, 'Ah, the one you've been playing detectives with. Let me deal with him. This is a matter of Security,' and made a dash for the front door. I ran after him and said, 'But I want to see him myself.' Then Lyn put a restraining hand on my arm and I suddenly felt I didn't really want the job of explaining everything to Tim, especially as he had warned me against bringing the police in – though it was Lyn who did that, and I really didn't blame her.

Lyn said, 'Let's find the clothes you need,' and we filled my one suitcase. I shall have to go back for more and I don't fancy it. I'd like never to see the flat again.

When Mike got back he said, 'That's all right. I'm sure your friend can be trusted not to talk. Incidentally, I've read one of his novels. It was very good. Now, let's get started on those tapes of yours.'

I said they could begin while I went down to have a word with Tim but Mike told me he'd already gone. 'He had an appointment. But he'll be in touch with you when he can. And he said to tell you he was sure you were now in good hands.' Mike looked slightly embarrassed, then added, 'Well, he really did say it.'

I felt flattened. Of course I've no claim on Tim and I know he has to earn his living, but I'd been counting on seeing him. I wonder if he's bowing out on me.

Mike decided not to start on the tapes until we were back here in Lyn's flat. He reckons the whole job will take quite five hours. He decided to start with the tape I recorded this morning, in case there's anything important I forgot to mention when he questioned me. The one tape I don't intend to hand over is this one, which describes him as ordinary. I doubt if anyone cares to be considered ordinary. Incidentally, he doesn't look as ordinary as he did. Once you like people, you see more in their faces. He and Lyn and a shorthand writer have been listening to the tapes ever since we got back here. I found I didn't want to listen with them. Lyn said, 'You go and do a nice recording.' Well, it's filling in the time until I go to the theatre. I'm to have police protection there, but only Rich will know. Mike feels he should. They're friends, actually; it was through Rich that Lyn met Mike.

Strange to be sitting here in my old bedroom in Lyn's flat. Do I wish I was back in those days? Oh, my God, I do! Do I wish I'd never met Roy? Yes. I suppose that means I've stopped caring for him. Could I be misjudging him? . . . It's no use. I can't get away from thinking that either he's guilty – of *something*; or he's an utter fool to have got himself involved in . . . well, whatever he has got involved in.

I wanted to leave a note at the flat for him to find when he gets back tomorrow, just telling him I'm with Lyn, but Mike advised against it – 'Just as well he shouldn't know.' Though he'll probably guess. Anyway, why should I bother? He didn't let me know where he was going. – Lyn's calling.

They broke off for us all to have an eggy tea. Lyn said the tapes were fascinating to listen to and Mike said, 'Seriously, Nan, you ought to write a book.'

I could never write a book. I couldn't have *written* the words I've talked. Perhaps I'll listen to them one day, all on my own. That night I first met Tim, I now haven't the faintest idea what I said about it. I do think Tim might have come up to the flat today and had just a word with me.

Signing off to go to the theatre now.

TAPE TWELVE

Friday, June 28th. 4 p.m.

Not a word from Tim. And presumably Roy hasn't yet returned to our flat. It's being watched and Mike has promised to let me know if Roy comes home.

Last night at the theatre: Mike had asked me not to tell anyone about my excitements and I didn't quite know what to say to my room-mate about my dodging the Count on Wednesday night. But she had to go 'on' which meant that she dressed down in her principal's dressing-room, and I only saw her to wish her luck and then, later, congratulate her.

Mike drove me to the theatre, then talked to Rich before going back to listen to more of my tapes. Rich spent quite a lot of the evening in my dressing-room. Naturally he's worried – he seems to think that one plain-clothes man wandering around the stage-door alley isn't enough protection. I ought to be locked up in some place entirely surrounded by the Army.

I can't myself believe that the Count or the horrible young man will make another attempt to kill me, but then I'd never have believed they would on Wednesday night, if it hadn't happened. If Cyprian Slepe instigated it, *why* did he? How can I be so important?

Rich wonders if I would be safer hidden away somewhere out of London, but I'd hate that. I want to be with people, all the time. For the few minutes I was alone in my dressing-room while Rich went back to his office I was absurdly nervous, and I was grateful to him for driving back to Lyn's flat with me. My detective drove us.

Mike and Lyn had finished listening to my tapes. Lyn again said they were fascinating and, 'Oh, my poor darling, what a time you've had.' Mike was extremely cagey. When I asked him if I'd supplied him with any clues he said, 'Possibly – when I've had time to read the transcription and think.' My guess is that he's completely bewildered, and who can blame him? But Lyn feels sure he has already set police machinery rolling. There are all sorts of enquiries he can make.

Lyn's rehearsing. I'd have liked to be there, but Mike asked me to stay here in her flat. It would be more difficult to keep an eye on me at the theatre – here, there's always some poor bored detective sitting outside the door. (Luckily the people who live in the flat opposite are away.) Anyhow I need to be here in case Mike telephones with news of Roy. And Tim might telephone.

I'm going to have a shot at tidying the kitchen, which is chaotic. That didn't matter much while Lyn was on her own as she seldom had any meal but breakfast here; but it now looks as if we shall have to eat in quite a lot – me, anyway, as Mike doesn't want me to go to restaurants at present; though surely no one would shoot me in full view of the public? Though I did see a television play in which someone who had become a menace to a Russian agent was poisoned in a restaurant. One knows so little about real life espionage that one's bound to be influenced by what one sees on TV. I've always told myself it was wildly exaggerated, but is it, I now wonder?

I shan't mind having my meals here. There's a womb-like cosiness about being shut up in this flat with a watchdog in a raincoat on the stairs. (I give him tea and coffee and feed him a bit.) What's more, I quite like cooking in Lyn's messy kitchen, whereas I loathed cooking in our quite tidy kitchen at the flat. This was partly because Roy was no fun to cook for. He didn't like my trying out new ideas, or any kind of snack. Him and his simple steaks! (Oh, God, I wish he'd come back – and yet I dread meeting him.) Lyn and I can still enjoy poached eggs on baked beans. Now to tackle that kitchen.

Saturday, June 29th, 2 p.m.
Lyn's gone to spend the day with her parents, who are now living in Brighton. She hasn't seen them since she got back from New York and felt she ought to, before she starts playing next week. She'll be back late tonight, I'm thankful to say. I shouldn't fancy being alone here all night, watchdog or no watchdog. Actually, I'm not enjoying being alone here during the day. It isn't that I'm frightened . . . exactly. It's just that I'm ill at ease unless I can talk to someone. That's why I'm talking to myself now.

Still no word from Tim. And Roy hadn't come back to the flat when Mike telephoned me around lunchtime. I wish Mike would talk more. Today I asked him if there was any news about *anything* and he merely said, 'I'll be in touch with you when there is.' Lyn and I have guessed every guess we can think of and are about to soar off into Science Fiction.

Nothing unusual at the theatre. My room-mate was playing again so wasn't there to ask awkward questions. Rich spent some time with me but we didn't talk about the melodrama I'm involved in. He thinks Lyn is going to be very good. We talked about his plans for me for the autumn, but I can't imagine ever getting out of the morass of worry I'm in. It's being so much in the dark that's driving me crazy.

Rich said——There's the telephone.

It was Roy, ringing from a call-box; he telephoned our flat and got no answer, so he hoped I might be at Lyn's. He said he'd got to see me quickly, would I come to the flat? I said no, I'd left it for good after what happened there. Perhaps he didn't know that someone had tried to kill me. He said, 'Good God, how could I know? But don't tell me now. I'll come to you, at once.'

I felt I couldn't face seeing him, and said, 'No, wait!' But he'd already rung off.

I've been trying to calm myself. Of course I must see him. I won't believe he had anything to do with the attacks on me. He'll be horrified about them. And this is my chance to convince him that Cyprian Slepe's dangerous. It must be Cyprian who's responsible for the Count's behaviour. But how about the other man? Roy knows him all right. But Roy wouldn't, he couldn't want me dead. Anyway, he's hardly likely to walk in and murder me, with a watchdog at the door. The watchdog . . . yes, I must cope with him.

I've been out and told the man I'm expecting my husband and it will be quite all right to let him in. I'm steadier now. I keep telling myself I ought to be relieved to have news of Roy. Soon he and I may have straightened everything out.

I keep thinking, thinking. There's the door bell.

Later.
Roy's been and gone. Already I'm wondering if I was mad to agree to what he wants. And I've given my word.

He looked terribly tired and strained. I've never seen him with such troubled eyes. I felt instantly sure he'd had nothing to do with the attacks on me. I relaxed, was glad to see him. I know I smiled.

He didn't smile back. Almost before I got the door closed he said, 'Who's that man out there?'

I said, quite lightly, 'Oh, that's my police protection.'

'You went to the police?'

'Lyn did. Please try to take it in, Roy. I've been in very real danger, twice. First, from the Count——'

He interrupted me. 'The Count? You must be out of your mind. He likes you and admires you.'

I started to tell him what happened at the theatre – and realised almost at once that he wasn't taking me seriously. Long before I reached the end he interrupted me.

'This is absolute rubbish. The poor old man just wanted to speak to you, to get you to go out with him. Oh, I daresay he overdid it but . . . Do you mean Lyn went to the police about this nonsense?'

'And about the other "nonsense". When I got home someone got into the flat – and then tried to shoot me. There's no doubt whatever. The police found the bullets.'

At last I'd made some impression. Roy said he was extremely sorry I'd had such a horrible experience, especially after I'd got myself so worked up about the Count – 'Not that there's any possible connection between the incidents.'

'But there is, Roy. They both emanate from Cyprian Slepe. Now for God's sake, listen.'

I began to tell him what Sylvia had overheard at Slepe, but he interrupted as soon as I reached the word 'eliminate'.

'He simply meant to keep you out of the work I'm sharing with him. And how could he be connected with an ordinary housebreaker?'

I shouted then. 'He wasn't an ordinary housebreaker. He was the man who came to the flat asking for you, the man with the long, dyed hair. I saw him clearly.'

'You made a mistake. These days there are any amount of men with long dyed hair.'

'I'm *sure*, Roy. Who *is* that man?'

'I told you. Just someone from Midhampton who cadges from me occasionally.'

'Was that what he was doing when you met him on the bridge in Regent's Park? Don't trouble to ask how I know that. I followed you there.'

The effect of this was shattering; Roy stared at me in horror, opened his mouth to speak but seemed unable to form words. Then he walked to the window and stood looking out. It must have been minutes before he turned to me again and spoke with surprising control.

What he said was: 'I beg you, for your own sake as much as for mine, not to question me about that, and to accept my word that it has nothing, nothing whatever to do with the present moment. I am in desperate trouble. Please believe I'm not minimising what you've been through, but I beg you to forget it for the moment and just listen to me, and help me if you can.'

He then told me that he has to go to Paris tonight. His work with Cyprian has struck a snag. 'The whole thing has been misconstrued. He and I must get to the Continent tonight and I want you to come with me.'

I said it was out of the question, I had my job at the theatre. He told me we needn't leave until after the show tonight and I could come back on Monday morning. 'All I'm asking of you is one day – tomorrow – so that I can explain everything.'

I said, 'Why can't you explain now?'

'Because there isn't the time. Already I ought to be somewhere else. And we've got to have some peace, without the fear of interruption. You may find it difficult to understand at first. Nan, our whole future's at stake – and not just *our* future; Cyprian's whole scheme's in jeopardy. And I now think that may be due to you. How much did you tell the police about the scheme?'

'I couldn't tell them what I didn't know. I simply let them listen to what I recorded about the weekend at Slepe.' Then I remembered the tapes had been disturbed. 'Perhaps you know what that was?'

He stared. 'How could I know? What did you record?'

I felt sure he wasn't pretending, so I went on quickly, 'Oh, just some impressions of the weekend, the house, the ruins, Celina's paintings. I don't know *anything* about Cyprian's scheme, and I've got to, now. Otherwise I won't even consider coming to Paris with you.'

'But I'm sworn to secrecy.'

'Then that will operate even if I come to Paris. And I can tell you now that I'm not going on with our life together unless I know what you're involved in. Unless you tell me *now*, we're finished.'

He said, 'Let me think, let me think,' then sat down at the table and put his head in his hands. At last he looked up and said, 'All right. There are certain things I can tell you.'

He told me that when Cyprian left England last year he got in touch with an organisation which is fighting to check the world-wide swing to Communism, which is far more advanced than most people suspect. 'It's all underground and has to be fought underground.'

He paused for a second and I slipped in, 'But Communism's no longer underground. If people want to fight it they can see what to fight. It's out in the open, legal, just taken for granted.'

'Which makes it infinitely more dangerous. People are losing their horror of it. Actually, it's not simple Marxism that's the real menace now – though that alone is responsible for most of our industrial unrest. What matters far more is that there are new and worse forms developing, such as anarchistic terrorism. Already there are brilliant men, historians, sociologists, who believe that some form of Marxism – possibly not yet invented – will eventually dominate the whole world. They see it as inevitable. But it's *not*, not if the underlying danger is fought now. The organisation Cyprian got in touch with is well established in Europe, but nothing's been done here in England. Cyprian was to take on the job and restore Slepe as the English headquarters. There are unlimited funds.'

I broke in, 'Cyprian hasn't enough funds to pay the local tradesmen, let alone restore Slepe.'

'There's been a delay over the transfer of currencies. All that would have to be ironed out. The scheme's backed by some of the richest men in the world.'

Something stirred in my memory. I remembered a book, a thriller, built round this very idea. It had seemed to me sheer fantasy and I still found it hard to believe in any such scheme. I asked Roy how he came into it.

'I've been working with Cyprian for weeks. That's why I've had to go so often to the Continent, to report to him on, well, some of my fellow-members of Parliament. One of his most important tasks will be to detect subversion.'

'But surely no member of Parliament——'

'Why not? There have been cases of espionage in the Civil Service, the Army, the Navy, and by the time these are discovered, the damage has been done. However, Cyprian's plan was preventative, to detect *potential* subversion. I've had to make friends with certain men who are living beyond their means and might be susceptible to temptation, form my opinion of them. I've found the work both difficult and distasteful – that's one reason why I've been so deeply worried. It's almost seemed like spying, though I've always known Cyprian planned to save such men from themselves. But what's the point in telling you all this, now the whole scheme's in ruins?'

'But what's gone wrong?'

'There must have been some leak about Cyprian's plans. Viewed from the wrong angle they could appear subversive. All we really know is that we've been warned by a loyal friend to get out of England tonight. And I beg you to come with me for just one day. You can come back on Monday.'

'And when will *you* come back?'

'Possibly quite soon, though I don't think Cyprian will. Oh, no doubt he'll be exonerated, but I don't see how he can go on with his scheme here. He may go to America where the organisation's already established. And I might feel I must go with him. So much depends on you now. We need to discuss our whole future. Surely you can give me one day?'

It flashed through my mind that this was my last chance to rescue Roy from Cyprian. He was talking wildly, but at least he was communicating with me again. Suppose I did go to Paris! I found I loathed the idea. Did this mean I no longer loved Roy? During the last days I had come to feel this – but even so, here was a man I *had* loved, now in desperate need of help.

He said, 'Please, Nan.' And there was something in his eyes and his voice that got right through to me. I said, 'All right. I'll come. I'll give you one day.'

His face lit up. 'Can I count on that? Will you promise?'

God help me, I did. He took me in his arms then, I think he meant to kiss me, but I just buried my head against his shoulder. I don't know why but I suddenly felt physical contact between us was impossible. I still don't know why.

He left then, after fixing where and what time I should meet him tonight. As I let him out of the flat I saw my watchdog. I'd forgotten about him, and I shall need to dodge him now as, much as I dread it, I have to go to the flat to get my passport. But it won't be difficult. I can get out of the kitchen by way of the tradesmen's stairs. (Mike had two bolts put on their door and the watchdog's on hand if anyone tries to break in.) Before I go I shall tell him I'm going to lie down, and ask him to see I'm not disturbed. I can be back long before it's time for him to escort me to the theatre. While I'm at the flat I can pick up a handbag large enough to take a nightdress and thin dressing-wrap. I mustn't take an overnight bag in case it alerts the watchdog. I can give him the slip tonight by going out through the front of the theatre while the curtain's still up. Poor man! But I can't fail Roy.

Suppose Mike rings up? I don't think he will, as it's

Saturday afternoon – even Special Branch men must have some private life; still, I'll leave the receiver off. I hope I've thought of everything . . . Lyn! But she won't be back until very late tonight, by which time I shall just about be meeting Roy. I'll leave a note telling her to listen to this recording . . . I keep remembering things Roy said, that I haven't recorded. There was something about his having been to Scotland with Cyprian, where some old laird had handed Cyprian a cheque for five thousand pounds and promised any amount more. Good God, is Cyprian some kind of trickster, a confidence man? Well, it's more likely than that he's a Communist spy.

Lyn, when you listen to this try to understand this is my last chance to save Roy. And don't worry. I'll be back on Monday. Make my apologies to Mike, but *please* don't let him hear the recording; anyway, not the part about Roy and about Cyprian's scheme. It sounds nonsense to me, but I suppose it just might be something genuine and worth while – and I'm already supposed to have wrecked it. Anyway, don't tell Mike about it unless I fail to come back – which I shan't. See you Monday.

TAPE THIRTEEN

Wednesday, July 3rd. 11.00 p.m.

On the way to the flat I remembered that Mike was having it watched. Would anyone try to stop me from going in? But as we drove into the square I couldn't see anyone outside the house. What I did see was a taxi, parked opposite. Was it Tim's? I'd wanted to see him, had been hurt because he hadn't got in touch with me, but I didn't want to see him now and have him asking me questions. I paid my fare before I got out of my taxi and then dashed up the steps. I hadn't actually seen Tim and – if he was there – he might not have seen me.

There was no one on guard outside the flat. I went in and quickly found my passport, also a large handbag and a thinner nightgown and dressing-wrap than I had back at Lyn's. I was just stuffing them all into the bag when Tim walked in. I'd left the front door open.

I just said brightly, 'Tim! How lovely to see you. I had to come in for a few things I need. Will you drive me back to Lyn's? We can talk on the way.'

He said, 'Right. Are you ready now?'

I said I was and we went downstairs and into his taxi. I expected him at least to ask me how I was, but he didn't say one word. I stared at the back of his head. Was he hurt, sulking? Or had Mike warned him off butting into things any more? Anyway, it was a relief that he didn't question me. I sat back and closed my eyes for a few moments. When I opened them we were driving through a street I didn't recognise. There was nothing unusual about that – Tim so often takes odd routes. Still, really to make conversation – I'd begun to feel sure he must be offended – I said, 'Where are we?'

He said, 'You'll see in a minute,' and then drove unusually fast. Soon we were on the Outer Circle of Regent's Park. I said, 'Surely this is miles out of our way?' He said nothing and a moment later turned into the mews where he lives.

I shouted, 'Tim, I asked you to take me to Lyn's.'

He said, 'So I will, but I've got to talk to you first.' Then he drew up, got out and opened the taxi door for me.

I felt my best plan was to take things calmly, so I just said, 'Well, for God's sake, why kidnap me?' and went into the house. As soon as we were in the sitting-room he said, brusquely, 'You've got a passport in that bag. I saw you put it there. Are you planning to leave England?'

I said, 'I'm simply going to spend a day in Paris with Roy.'

'Have you informed Special Branch?'

'Not yet. I've only just decided to go. Anyway, why need I inform anyone? I shall be back on Monday.'

'You will not,' said Tim. 'You'll probably be dead by Monday. Though you may be allowed to live a little longer provided you accept exile with Roy.'

I said angrily, 'Tim, stop it. This isn't one of your thrillers.'

'No woman in any of my thrillers has ever behaved as idiotically as you're behaving now. Didn't being fired at on Wednesday night convince you that you're up against criminals?'

'Roy's no criminal. Oh, I know he's in trouble now, but it's due to some misunderstanding and I've got to let him explain. That's why I'm going with him and nothing you can say will stop me.'

Tim's manner changed. It had been almost bullying. Now he became gentle, persuasive. 'Sit down and listen – please, if you want to stay alive. I'm not accusing Roy of being a criminal, though it's hard to believe he doesn't know he's associating with one. Among other things, Cyprian Slepe's a would-be murderer. That man who fired at you was his hired assassin.'

'Even if that's true, I'm sure Roy doesn't know it – and neither do you, Tim, not really. And now I'm going back to Lyn's.' What was uppermost in my mind now was to get back. Already I'd been away longer than I'd intended. In half-an-hour it would be time for the watchdog to drive me to the theatre for the first show. He'd probably hammer on the door to wake me.

Tim said, 'I do know. Well, you'd better have the facts about me, at last. I'm not just a sympathetic taxi-driver who's accidentally got involved in your affairs. I was watching your husband long before you asked me to follow him to Regent's Park. A fellow M.P. whom he'd questioned most ineptly, alerted us.'

'Do you mean you're something to do with the police?'

'Not the police. Call it Security. I'm desperately sorry to have to tell you, but I must convince you I know what I'm talking about.'

I felt quite sick with shock. All his warmth and kindness had been a trick. I said bitterly. 'Then no doubt you've been spying on me, too. Was it you who disturbed my tapes? Perhaps you've listened to them. Have you a key to the flat?'

He said he'd had one for weeks and also a key to the house. 'Yes, I've listened to your recordings. I suppose I must have been too shattered on Wednesday night to put them back carefully. You never told me about Cyprian's decision to have you eliminated. That word from him was deadly sinister. It was late when I got as far as that. I drove to the theatre to warn you, but found it closed. So I drove back to the square. Your flat was in darkness so I went into the house; I found the door of your flat bolted. I thought you might be dead inside. Then I remembered the fire-escape and got onto it from the floor below. Once inside the flat, I telephoned Special Branch. We didn't want them in on it yet – we weren't ready. But once you were threatened—'

I said, 'Sorry if I've got under your feet.'

'Mike rang Lyn that night, hoping you'd be there, (as you were) and told her to go on getting facts out of you and ring him in the morning.'

I'd heard the telephone when I was in the bathroom but Lyn had told me it was a wrong number. I said now, 'When you asked me to make those recordings were you already planning to listen to them?'

He said no, he'd genuinely thought they might help me, but he'd soon seen that they might help him, too. 'Not that they did, except to make me more and more suspicious of your husband. Oh, my dear, if only I could convince you that I haven't simply been hypocritical.'

'Well, you can't. But don't let that depress you. Obviously your job had to come first.'

It's a strange feeling when great liking turns suddenly to hatred. And I didn't only hate Tim on my own account. I was overcome with guilt because I had, it seemed, handed Roy over to him on a plate. Well, I'd try to make up for that now. I went on, 'I'm going now. And it may interest you to know that nothing you've said is going to stop me meeting Roy after the show.'

'Where are you meeting him?'

'In Trafalgar Square, by the fountains. They'll be handy for me to fall into when he strangles me.'

'He won't lay a finger on you,' said Tim. 'But others may. Don't you realise how simple it would be for someone to shove a needle into you? You'd slump down, kind people would send for an ambulance to take you to a hospital, where you'd be found dead on arrival.'

I told him not to talk nonsense. 'Anyway, it's no use, I

promised.'

He sighed heavily, then spoke gently. 'All right, I'll drive you. Just one minute. There should be a message from my help.'

He went into the kitchen. I guessed he might go on trying to persuade me when he returned and I wondered if I should bolt, while I had the chance. But I feared I should have difficulty in picking up a taxi and I was dead set on getting back to Lyn's before the watchdog discovered I wasn't there. So I stayed put. Tim was gone longer than I expected. I called out, 'Please hurry,' and then he came back. Just as I expected, he returned to the attack, begging me to listen.

I said, 'No, no, no!' and made for the door.

'Well, if you won't, you won't,' said Tim, and followed me. The next instant I felt a sharp prick in my arm and then a black curtain rose upwards and blotted the world out.

When I recovered consciousness the room was in darkness. I was lying down – for a moment I thought I was in bed and had wakened in the middle of the night. Then I saw a pale upright oblong of light, and then memory came stealing back. The light was in Tim's kitchen and I was lying on his sofa. Had I been asleep? Had I fainted? Then I was fully awake – or almost. I remembered Tim jabbing me in the arm but I still wasn't capable of reasoning, I'd no idea why he'd done it. And when I heard sounds in the kitchen and guessed he must be in there I was terrified.

I must have made some sound because a man's figure appeared at the kitchen door and a voice said softly, 'Are you awake?'

I couldn't see the man's face because all the light was behind him, but I was instantly sure it wasn't Tim. The head was small and neat, with no Simple Simon hair. And the voice wasn't Tim's. I closed my eyes quickly but he must have seen they'd been open because he came in, switched on the light and said, 'There's absolutely no need to be frightened'. Then he knelt beside me – and my God, it *was* Tim, with a short haircut. I stared and stared, then said idiotically, 'You're wearing a wig.'

He laughed and said, 'No, the other was a wig.'

'And why are you talking in that voice?'

He was speaking in an ultra upper-class voice, the kind of voice Lyn calls '*high posh*'.

He said, 'It's *my* voice. And I can only get away from it by completely playing a character part. I told you I'd been an actor.'

'But why get away from it?'

He said that his normal voice and appearance were not like those of most taxi-drivers and he didn't want to be in any way noticeable. 'But I can't keep up that nonsense with you. Though I suspect you preferred me as I was.'

This was putting it mildly. Compared with my kind, sloppy Tim, with his mouth full of pebbles, I found this elegant stranger chilling, but at least I'd stopped being frightened of him. I said, 'What did you do to me to knock me out?'

'Nothing that has done you the slightest harm. How do you feel?'

Actually I felt perfectly well but I just said, 'Oh, I'm more or less all right. And I'm going back to Lyn's. No, I'll go to the theatre first.'

He said he didn't advise that as it was one a.m.

'But . . . Good God, you must have put me out for hours and hours. I've missed meeting Roy. I've failed him.'

'That,' said Tim, 'was the object of the exercise. But he doesn't know you failed him. He wasn't there.'

'Then where is he?'

'My guess is that he's got out of England with the Slepes, but I don't know for certain. Incidentally, he may never have intended to meet you. But someone else may have been waiting for you, to bump you off.'

'I swear Roy would never have been a party to that. And

why should anyone want to kill me?'

'I just don't know. There are many things I don't know and most of what I do know, I'm not allowed to tell you. So please lay off questioning me. Now I must telephone Mike to say you're awake. The telephoning I've done on your behalf tonight, my girl! Mike, your friend Gott at the theatre, and Lyn eventually. She came back earlier than she expected and relayed your recording to Mike. But it didn't say where you were meeting Roy.'

'And I told you without giving it a thought. If Roy had been arrested it would have been my fault.'

While Tim telephoned Mike, I looked round the gleaming little sitting-room thinking of the first time I came there, less than three weeks earlier. (Just three weeks ago today, actually.) When Tim came back I said, 'I suppose this jewel-box room is your own?'

He said no, it really had been lent to him. 'When I rent places they're apt to be bed-sitting-rooms in sleazy districts. Mike's coming round to collect you. Now I'll give you some coffee. I got it all ready as I was expecting you to wake up.'

While we were drinking it Tim said, 'Oh, my dear, dear Nan – remember telling me I could call you that? – if only I could help you! Do you feel desperately unhappy about that bastard of a husband of yours?'

'I haven't written him off as a bastard yet. Oh, I suppose he must be, well, some kind of a criminal or else a gullible fool. But there *could* be some kind of an explanation. As for how I feel, how can I tell – when I'm still so much in the dark?'

'Do you still hate me? You did when you woke up, didn't you?'

'A bit perhaps, because of the deception. But it was more, really, because you weren't *my* Tim. I'll probably get over it.'

But I wonder if I ever shall, quite. Though I do feel that, as well as doing his job, he was always trying to help me and protect me.

When Mike came he brought my watchdog with him. I told him I was sorry to have tricked him and he was very nice about it, but I shouldn't think he'd ever trust me again. I'm thankful that he didn't get into trouble.

I'm still having police protection. I don't know why. Mike won't tell me anything – he and Tim could do a double turn as oysters. Though Mike did telephone on Sunday morning to let me know Roy and the Slepes *had* left England.

I said, 'What about the Count and the man who tried to shoot me?'

'I can't tell you anything about them,' said Mike.

Lyn opened as leading lady on Monday, with great success. You'd think my troubles might have had a shattering effect on her, but she was steady as a rock. We're trying to live as normally as possible, but you can't really feel normal with a relay of watchdogs always around. It's not *knowing* anything that's so maddening. Well, thank God for Lyn – and for Rich. He wanted to take us both out to supper after Lyn's first night but Mike was against it, so we had a party here at Lyn's and gave the watchdog champagne.

I'm going to live from day to day. But shall I ever feel – well, in the clear again? How can I stop worrying about Roy? And the truth is – I might as well face it – I'm continually afraid.

TAPE FOURTEEN

Tuesday, July 23rd. 12.15 p.m.

When I last recorded, almost three weeks ago, I expected to record again soon. But talking to Lyn is a substitute for recording and I'm only talking to myself again now because there's something I want to get clear, all on my own. I'm still at Lyn's. We talk very vaguely about getting a better flat, but we shall never find anything as central – or as cheap, as this. Not that we're worried about money at present. Rich has extended the run of the play and is already casting the new play in which we're both to have parts. And I may get a television series. I'm reasonably cheerful, mainly because Rich and Tim and, of course, Lyn are so good to me. But I'm still in the dark about – well, practically everything.

The only new development is that, about a week ago, my police protection was withdrawn, but Mike wouldn't say why. I gather the stone wall all my questions come up against is that all powerful word, Security. Incidentally, there's been no word in the papers about Roy, or the Slepes. No doubt Security prevents it.

I've stuck to my determination to live from day to day, thankful for friends, the theatre, meals, any little pleasure. I'd become – well, almost – resigned to not knowing the true facts about Roy, or where he is, or what's happened to him. I've worked hard at shutting my mind to thoughts of him. And now, this morning, out of the blue, there comes a letter from him.

He and the Slepes are in Buenos Aires – or rather, they were; he says, 'We shall have left before you get this.' I gather that Cyprian's anti-Communist scheme is arousing much interest in South America. 'He now sees that England, where he was so cruelly misjudged, is hopeless as a base. He must work *internationally*. And mercifully we're not short of money. Apart from what Cyprian was able to bring, funds are flowing in.'

All this part of the letter infuriated me. Roy seemed as obsessed as ever with Cyprian and quite oblivious of me. And then I came to the last pages of the letter – all written in Roy's tiny, print-script writing. It said:

'There is something I hoped you need never know, but I now feel that telling you may be my one way of helping you. When I was a very young man I had an affair with a girl in my father's factory. She soon told me she was going to have a child and persuaded me to marry her, secretly – I did not dare tell my father. There was no child and, a few months later, the girl disappeared. I ought to have traced her and got free of her, but this would have meant my father finding out, so I let things slide. Some ten years later a man who said he was living with her wrote to say she was ill and in need of help. So I sent some money. A few months later the man wrote to say she was dead. He asked me to help him. It was a reasonable letter and the amount he asked for was small, so I sent it and heard no more from him.

I then felt quite free and, when we married, my only illegality was that I did not describe myself as a widower. Had I done so it would have meant difficult explanations to my mother.'

After that, the letter is full of excuses, about his mother's state of health, the rigidity of his upbringing, etc. He keeps shying away from what he now feels he has to tell me, but I think I've got a reasonably clear picture of the facts.

In the Spring, after he was in touch with the Slepes again, he took to going for long morning walks. (I remember this.) He was worried about what Cyprian was asking him to do, wanted to think things out. One day he walked right across Regent's Park and ended up on the bridge where we first met. Here he was joined by the man with long, dyed hair. He'd had some past connection with Midhampton, recognised Roy and struck up a conversation, in the course of which he said he knew Roy's first wife.

Roy said his first wife was dead. The man said he'd seen her quite recently, in Birmingham. Roy spoke of the letter about her death he had received all those years ago. The man said the letter-writer had probably been slung out by Roy's wife and had seen a way of getting money. But alive she certainly was – the man supplied her address.

He had known of Roy's marriage to me – there was quite a bit in the papers about it – but, as the woman had been living for years with someone supposed to be her husband, he had taken it for granted that there had been a divorce. Now he realised that Roy, though accidentally, had married me bigamously, and the idea of blackmail was born then and there.

Roy succumbed because of me, because of his position as an M.P. and because of the Slepes. And the word blackmail was not mentioned; the man merely asked for a little help. But in a couple of weeks he wrote again, demanding more. Roy had driven to Birmingham, parked near the woman's house and seen her come out. She was alive all right. So again he paid the blackmailer. That night in June when I overheard the telephone conversation was the fourth demand. Again he met the man on the bridge, but hadn't enough money to satisfy him and had to promise more. That night I saw the man in the square he was waiting to get it.

By now Roy had begun to think the situation was hopeless. The man's demands and recklessness were increasing. But there was no further demand until after our weekend at

Slepe. Then the man accosted Roy outside the House and, in despair, Roy revealed the whole truth to Cyprian.

Roy writes: 'Imagine my astonished gratitude when he was instantly sympathetic, assured me *he* would meet the man on the bridge that night (as I had agreed to) and would cope with him. God knows what he did but, before we left for Scotland on the Wednesday, he told me I need worry no more. Then, on our return to London, we learned that Cyprian's whole scheme had been misinterpreted, and we must at once get out of England. I meant to tell you the whole truth when we were in Paris but, in the end, Cyprian made me see that I must not meet you that night and the best thing I could do for you is to set you free – which you legally are.'

Cyprian, Cyprian, Cyprian! All the same, when I finished this part of the letter, I felt desperately sorry for Roy. What he must have gone through! But as I read on, my pity dwindled. The rest of the letter is just a hymn of praise to Cyprian and his plan to save the world. Roy says not one word about his cutting his political career short, about his family business, financial arrangements . . . Well, perhaps there's no reason why he should tell me anything of this kind, or show concern for my future. He knows I can earn my own living. Presumably the letter is just to set me free. He doesn't explain why the blackmailer tried to kill me – or why the Count wanted to.

Lyn's gone to lunch with Mike and – in the light of this letter, which I've let her read – will make another attempt to get more information out of him. And I shall try with Tim. I've asked him to lunch with me here.

3.00 p.m.

Tim's been and gone. I found he already knew that Roy and the Slepes were in South America. He did not know about Roy being married and blackmailed, any more than Mike did. Tim said it explained quite a lot, but he wouldn't tell me what it explained, or answer any of my questions. He simply said it was still a matter of Security. At last I shouted, 'God damn and blast Security! Am I to spend the rest of my life not understanding the nightmare I've lived through? And how do I know that the blackmailer won't have another shot at killing me, not to mention the Count?'

Then Tim sprang up in the middle of a mouthful of the lunch I'd cooked for him. He said, 'I've just thought. There *is* one way I might help you, but it may be too late. I'll try, anyway – now!'

I begged him to finish his lunch first and he did just shovel in what was on his plate. Then he dashed off, having told me to wait by the telephone. 'But don't count on anything. Even if I'm not too late, it may be out of the question.'

He's now been gone over an hour. The damn telephone's rung twice; once it was a wrong number and once it was Lyn, reporting she'd got nothing out of Mike, was going shopping and would be back for our pre-theatre meal. I didn't tell her about Tim, in case it comes to nothing.

There's the telephone again.

It was Tim, telling me to meet him on – of all places – the bridge in Regent's Park. I said, 'Why there, for God's sake?' He said, 'No time to explain. Just be there, by four o'clock.' Then he rang off.

Why, why, that particular place? I should have thought Tim would guess it might upset me. I'm off.

5.45 p.m.
I got to the Outer Circle a bit early, paid my taxi off at Clarence Gate and walked slowly towards the bridge. It was a lovely afternoon, sunny, windless, peaceful. I reckoned up: it's just on six weeks since that night I followed Roy.

As I drew nearer the bridge I saw there were two men standing on it. One of them was Tim – the 'posh' Tim, as he had been at lunch, though he still wears his wig when he's being a taxi driver. He was talking to the other man, whose face I couldn't see. Then Tim saw me and waved, and the other man looked in my direction.

I stopped dead. Surely it couldn't be——? The next instant I was sure. The man standing beside Tim was the Count.

For one wild second – no doubt it shows what state of mind I've been in for weeks – I wondered if Tim had gone over to the enemy and he and the Count now intended, jointly, to murder me. Should I turn and run? Then I controlled myself. I was sure Tim would never want to hurt me. I went on walking towards the bridge. Soon I was near enough to see that the Count was smiling broadly. Very debonair he was looking, with a flower in his button-hole.

They both came to meet me. Then, while the Count warmly shook hands, Tim said, 'Now I shall leave you. And I do assure you, dear Nan, that you are in safe hands.' He was off before I could say a word.

The Count gently steered me towards two chairs on the grass saying, 'The bridge makes a charming meeting place but one cannot indefinitely stand up.' He then told me the botanical name of the plant Roy and I called the giant cow-parsley, but I don't remember it.

Once we were seated the Count said, 'My dear Miss Sheldon – Tim tells me that is now your legal name, for which we must surely be thankful. He has also told me that you actually feared I wished to assassinate you that night in the theatre. How truly dreadful! I was simply trying to warn you not to go home, where – I very well knew – you *would* be in danger of assassination. Again and again I begged you to stop and listen. And on the rooftop I shouted, "Don't go home!"'

I said, 'I only heard, "Don't go." And anyway, why couldn't Tim have explained to me what you were really trying to do? Didn't he know?'

'He did, indeed. But he was determined to preserve what is known as "my cover".'

'Do you mean you do the same kind of Security work that Tim does?'

'Not quite the same. In my case, it is essential that I should not be found out.'

'Are you a spy?'

'A Secret Agent would describe me better. And even that is too much of a simplification.'

My mind took a leap. 'Are you a *Double* Agent?'

He smiled. 'Are there such people? Surely most of us to whom that description is applied are definitely on one side or the other . . . in the long run. Of course some of us occasionally "turn" – often through force of circumstances – and then we favour the side we have "turned" to – or do we only appear to? And quite often we "turn" back again – which is extremely confusing for our masters, who will put up with quite a lot from valuable men. I, personally, have never "turned" ideologically, though I do sometimes award little gifts of information to . . . let us say, the side which *misguidedly* believes it is employing me. One likes occasionally to play God, and do exactly as one pleases. But I mustn't confuse you. Now let me tell you all I feel I may.'

He said that when the Slepes left England last year, Cyprian really did believe there was some enormously rich secret organisation dedicated to the overthrow of Communism, which he hoped to become part of – to his great financial advantage. But he never discovered anything on the scale he had expected and nobody was willing to finance him. Then, at a time when his own resources were running out, he met the Count, who began by feeling sympathy for him.

'You see, my dear, having long ago lost my own ancestral home in Poland, I could understand his feeling for his –

which sounded much better than it actually is. A truly repulsive house.'

One day Cyprian announced that he would willingly sell his soul to the devil, as the ancestor who built Slepe is alleged to have done, in order to get money to restore it. The Count playfully suggested that the Russians might stand in as a substitute for the devil. Cyprian took the idea seriously, said the world was finished anyway, and from now on he was only going to consider his own personal fortunes. It was a mixture of 'If you can't beat 'em, join 'em,' and, from now on, 'Evil be thou my Good.' In fact, roll out enough Russian cash and Cyprian Slepe's enormously valuable services are yours.

And, said the Count, those services did look valuable to the Russians. Cyprian's aristocratic background, his reputation as right of right wing, his presumed circle of friends . . . oh, yes, indeed, Cyprian was a catch as a traitor and, far more so, as a recruiter of British traitors. The Count was delighted with the whole scheme – 'You see, my dear, it appealed to my vicious delight in playing God. I would let that scheme go just as far as I wished, and no further.'

Roy, as a member of Parliament, was now a valuable asset. He was sent for by Cyprian, forgiven for marrying me and given details of the scheme – but told it was Cyprian's share of the world-plan to defeat Communism. Roy believed Cyprian was out, not to recruit British traitors, but to unearth potential ones.

Here the Count interrupted his narrative for a little dissertation on the relationship between Roy and Cyprian. With old-fashioned reticence he gradually explained that he had at first thought there might be 'something a little unnatural between them – I believe the modern word for this is "queer". But I am sure there is nothing . . . shall we say "physical". Cyprian, who is emotionally an iceberg, has a great mental need for a devoted disciple. And poor Roy, who is . . . possibly a little immature for his age, has need of a father figure. It's pleasant to think that he has never been disillusioned. Cyprian is now right of right wing again and, as far as Roy is concerned, always has been.'

Back on his story again the Count said, 'When the Slepes returned to England, I intended the scheme to go forward for some time longer. But during that weekend when I had the pleasure of meeting you I realised Cyprian was on the edge of megalomania, and his hatred and jealousy of you were completely out of hand. Up till then, I had usually acted as his go-between with the Russians but he had one contact – whom he approached, the day after we returned to London, with a demand that you should be physically eliminated. I don't deny that our Russian friends can be ruthless, but the assassination of the wife of an M.P., for no important reason, did not appeal to them. Cyprian was very firmly snubbed.'

And that was the day Roy told him about being blackmailed. Cyprian must have been enchanted to learn I wasn't legally married to Roy, and even more enchanted when – having promised Roy to cope – he met the blackmailer, who would no doubt have been prepared to murder his own mother if paid enough. Late on the Wednesday afternoon Cyprian informed the Count that arrangements had now been made for my elimination. 'You see, my dear,' said the Count, 'he saw himself as a mediaeval tyrant with a gang of bullies in his service. He had now recruited his first bully.'

The deed was planned for that night and was to look like the work of a housebreaker. After happily informing the Count, Cyprian removed himself and Roy to Scotland, where a gullible old laird obliged with a large cheque (to fight Communism!) which Cyprian cashed before he finally bolted. The Count set out to warn me at the theatre.

'Imagine my panic when you eluded me and went off to certain danger. After I got down from the roof by the fire-escape, I got your address from a telephone book in a kiosk, and tried to ring you up. I could get no answer so I drove to your flat. When I got there you had vanished but Tim, whom I know very well, was there and we pooled our information.'

After that, everything had to end, to the regret of both sides, 'And mine, personally,' said the Count. 'It was the kind of elaborate fantasy which appealed to my Russian friends, and my English friends hoped to unearth some potentially dangerous characters. And I should have had the fun of pulling the strings. But one cannot work with megalomaniacs. When Cyprian returned from Scotland I had to say, "Fly at once! All is discovered." So he and his sister and Roy made a dramatic escape – by helicopter, I believe. Actually they could have gone any way they pleased as no one would have tried to stop them. They hadn't *yet* done anything criminal. True, Cyprian had tried to instigate your murder but there was no proof of that. Are there any questions you would like to ask me?'

'What about the man who Cyprian hired to kill me? Is he still around?'

'He was a wanted criminal and has been arrested for a crime of violence he committed some time ago. Tim, who saw him clearly that night he met Roy on the bridge here, has been able to identify him. He will undoubtedly get a long sentence.'

So that was why my police protection was called off; not, anyway, that the man would want to kill me unless paid for it.

I thanked the Count for telling me so many things which must surely be connected with his own security. He smiled and said he hardly thought I would give him away to his Russian friends and, even if I did, he doubted if it would greatly matter. 'You see, I do think of them as friends and I perform many genuine services for them. They may indeed know to whom I owe my first loyalty and just accept it. The rules of our strange game are complicated. Still, one should preserve secrecy when possible. But when Tim explained to me about your position I felt you were entitled to a little enlightenment.'

I thanked him again and then said, '*Is* it a game you play, you and Tim and others like you?'

He smiled again. 'In a way, perhaps. I certainly enjoy it. But it's a dangerous game with severe penalties for losing. However, I'm in no trouble at present. My Russian friends are grateful to me for pulling them out of what might have been a costly and embarrassing mistake. In fact, I'm starting for the Continent tonight on another little ploy for them. And as I still have much to do . . . See, the loyal Tim is waiting for you in his taxi.'

I looked towards the Outer Circle. Tim was at the place where he had been the night he first drove me to Regent's Park. As we walked across the grass towards him I asked the Count if he thought Cyprian would ever return.

'I doubt it,' said the Count. 'He has nothing to return to. And he has been badly scared.'

'What will happen to Slepe Hall? Will the local authorities take it over?'

'Such matters take time. And ruin comes swiftly to long-neglected houses.'

I remembered Cyprian at dinner, saying that rather than open Slepe to the public he would leave it to moulder – 'walls crumbling, giant weeds obscuring the broken windows, the great staircase falling . . .' I said, 'I suppose Celina's pictures will eventually rot. To me, she has a touch of genius.'

'And so has Cyprian. Genius and megalomania often go together. The details of his scheme to save the world from Communism, which he invented to amuse himself and impress poor Roy, were unbelievably clever. Well, who knows? Perhaps he will eventually create his own organisation and return at the head of an army of followers. I wonder what shirts they will wear? Shot silk perhaps.'

We reached Tim in his taxi. He had put on his wig. The

Count smiled on it benignly, 'Such fun! Real cloak and dagger work. Alas, I am hopeless at disguises.' He declined Tim's offer to drive him anywhere and said he wished to explore Regent's Park more fully. 'It might be a useful place to meet people.' He turned to me. 'But I shall arrange no meetings on your bridge. I feel that belongs to you – and to the past. Very definitely to the past. And now au revoir, my dear Nan Sheldon. I shall hope, on my return to England, to see you adorning the London stage.'

He left us swiftly, crossing the grass of the park at a brisk pace. As we stood looking after him I said to Tim, 'Was it his idea he should meet me on the bridge?'

Tim nodded. 'He thought it might give a kind of shape to your recent anxieties and finish them off for good.'

'How very perceptive of him.'

'You do realise the risk he took by telling you what he is?'

'He said he wasn't in any danger.'

'All double agents are.'

'He said he wasn't really a double agent.'

'Ah,' said Tim, dryly.

We got into the taxi. Tim said he would drive me to Lyn's, and then go on to ply his trade. 'I really do ply it, you know. Would you like another picnic on Sunday?'

'Love it. And you don't have to wear your wig. I'm used to you without it now.'

'Good,' said Tim, and then, a moment later, 'How discreet can you be about what the Count told you?'

'I shan't even tell Lyn. I've no desire to. All that matters to me now is that I'm safe and free.'

And now, recording those words, I realise I truly am free. It's not so much that I've got over caring for Roy as that he's ceased to exist for me. It's . . . as if I never knew him. I suddenly remember Celina calling her portrait of him 'Tabula Rasa' . . . something empty, erased. I find it hard to believe he's there, in South America, a real, live person. I don't want to believe it – though God knows I wish him well.

I shall try to forget my life with him, to erase it, as he most strangely has become erased for me. I'll think myself back into the days when Lyn and I left drama school and set out on our way. I don't know how much talent I have but surely the driving force that brought me to London is still there? I'll make something of my life yet.

Lyn's not back yet. She doesn't know I went out to meet the Count and I'll make sure she never listens to this recording. She always says she finds it hard to be discreet – and why burden her with secrecy? Especially as I don't want to talk any more about it all, not even to this tape-recorder. And Tim says that, later, Mike can tell her my would-be assassin was undoubtedly hired by Cyprian and is now safely in jail. That'll clear quite a lot up for her.

I'll start getting our 'high tea' ready. And then we'll be off to the theatre. I might give Rich a hint that this is a night for champagne. Dear Rich – and dear Tim. But what matters most to me now is that wonderful word 'Free!'